# After Io

Elliott Wink

This novel is a work of fiction. Names, characters, businesses, places, events, and incidents are either the products of the author's imagination or used in a fictitious manner. Any resemblance to actual persons, living or dead, or actual events is purely coincidental.

*For my mother, who has always been my biggest fan.*

## Contents

## Chapter 1 - 05.08.2231
## 22:40, Earthtime

Bryn issued a mayday call ten hours after she killed her captain.

Her fingernails were stained with dry blood where she hadn't scrubbed thoroughly enough, and her jumpsuit was torn and discolored from the incident. She angled the camera so all they would be able to see was her head and the very tips of her shoulders. Then she angled herself to hide the little cuts on the left side of her face. She'd pulled her hair back into a tight bun and pinched her right cheek to bring blood flowing back into the pale, thin skin.

She tried to make herself look more normal—maybe even attractive. It certainly wouldn't hurt her chances to look attractive, but normal, calm and collected were all of the utmost importance. No one ever responded to a mayday call from a crazy person;

outer space was already hostile enough without the chaos of unstable people. To have even the smallest chance of rescue, Bryn needed to seem utterly normal. Upstanding. Someone worth saving.

She needed to seem like someone who didn't know anything she shouldn't.

She wasn't sure she was worth saving. But there was an impulse, strong and involuntary like a gag reflex, that rejected the possibility of her own death. So here she was, about to film a commercial trying to convince any other ship within three astronomical units to spend the money in fuel to come save her pathetic life.

Bryn straightened her shoulders and softened the expression on her face. She breathed in to steady herself and read off the script she had written only minutes ago.

"Mayday, mayday, this is Bryn Michaels of the Persika. Two days ago, our ship lost power while on route from Io to Ligon Station after colliding with an unidentified object. Life support systems in all parts of the ship except the cockpit failed immediately and three of our crew died shortly after impact."

Bryn paused and blinked several times, trying to remember what expression she should have on her face so they did not know the next sentences out of her mouth were egregious lies. "My captain passed away from resulting wounds earlier today after trying to make repairs on the ship. I am the only surviving crew member of the Persika and I do not have the ability to repair the ship myself. I have sixteen hours of oxygen remaining." Bryn looked down at her hands, split and blood red, and then back into the camera. Tears welled in her eyes. "Please come save me," she said, her voice cracking.

Bryn turned off the camera and encoded her coordinates into the data before sending it out into the void. She did not watch it; it was either good enough or it wasn't, but she wasn't recording it again. It took all of her energy to maintain her demeanor the first time; she knew she would only come off more erratic and detached each time she read through the contrived speech.

For a moment Bryn stayed put, half expecting a message back instantly—someone willing and ready to rescue her. She sat in front of the message board for nearly thirty minutes, unmoving, until she realized that there was no use in waiting. When she finally stood up, she went straight for the sink. Bryn scrubbed her hands for ten minutes, getting between every line on her knuckles and deep into the cuticles of her fingernails to strip away every speck of blood on her skin. When she was finally satisfied, her skin was so raw that it nearly bled itself. But Bryn thought that might be okay; blood would be fine if it was her own. She had plenty to spare.

Laid out on the floor, amid all the other items she had pulled out of the cabinets, Bryn managed to find a long sleeve shirt. She pulled down the top of her ripped jumpsuit and tied it around her waist. The shirt was a bit snug, but it was crisp and warm. Bryn began to feel clean again. She felt her heart rate steadying as she breathed in deep, but the tinge of iron in the air reminded her of how unclean she was, no matter how much she scrubbed her hands. Bryn turned back to the center of the cockpit where her captain's body lay slumped in her chair.

From behind, it almost looked like Amai was sleeping. Her thick black hair rose up above the top of the headrest, and her left arm was still positioned on the armrest. But the pool of dark blood directly underneath her was unmistakable, and even from a distance someone would know that Amai was dead.

It made her uncomfortable; Bryn would have been lying if she said otherwise. But there was no better option. She couldn't remove her from the cockpit because she couldn't open the doors. And even in death, Amai was still her captain. She wouldn't stuff her body into a cabinet or a corner, just so she didn't have to look at what she'd done. Amai deserved better than that. Besides, Bryn did not have any intention of hiding her actions, at least not after she'd been rescued. She did what she had to do. They would all understand that.

However, Bryn didn't have a good excuse for leaving Amai's blood pooled on the ground. She left it simply because she couldn't bear to get any more on herself. And all of the readings indicated that the artificial gravity would hold for at least twice as long as the oxygen, at which point she'd either be rescued or dead.

With freshly scrubbed hands and a clean shirt, Bryn sat in the only unoccupied chair in the cockpit, immediately adjacent to her dead captain. She could reach out and touch Amai if she wanted, but instead she pulled her feet up to her chest and stared forward at the stars.

## Chapter 2 - 5.04.2231
## 06:07, Earthtime

"Everything loaded?" Amai asked when she found her crew at breakfast. She grabbed a roll off Ezreal's plate and sat down with them.

They all nodded, but Bryn was the only one to actually answer. "All loaded. It took three hours to get the drill secured last night, but Tina managed to make it happen."

Tina didn't look up from her eggs, but she held up a peace sign with her left hand.

"Great," Amai said, forcing a smile. She picked off small chunks of the roll but didn't eat any of it. Instead, she dropped them onto the table in front of her, creating a little mountain of crumbs. She looked around at her crew, five in total: Bryn, Tina, Ezreal, Maverik, and Gabe. Bryn was her pilot, Tina was the mechanic, and the other three were the workers assigned to her by the Company to actually do the drilling and secure the payload. Amai had worked with Ezreal before, but Maverik and Gabe were new. Tina and Bryn were her personal crew—they were as much a part of the ship as the engines or the computer, and in that way they were irreplaceable.

"Well," Amai said, brushing her pile of crumbs onto the floor. "We're scheduled to take off in three hours, so I expect to see you all in two."

They all nodded again, still occupied by their food, and Bryn gave her a small smile. Amai couldn't think of anything else to say, so she left them to their food and made her way to the ship. The rest of the crew would take their time at breakfast and then spend their remaining minutes ambling around the station—perusing through shops for things they didn't want or chatting up the locals—doing anything to kill time away from the ship. They saw the station as freedom and the ship as a confinement. In a way, Amai understood them; the ship was small, and once they left the station there was nowhere to go until they docked again. But to Amai, her ship was home. Where her crewmates may have felt confined, Amai felt comfort. So, she spent the hours before departure straightening up the cockpit and laying in her bed, reading some old books from the home world.

Once the rest of the crew arrived, it was routine as usual. The flight checks and departure went off without a hitch, and they were on their way to Io to mine platinum. When Amai first got her ship, she spent a few years ferrying supplies and refugees to new stations; she'd taken a vow to use her good fortune ethically: to help people. But the upkeep was far more expensive than she'd expected, and Amai found quickly that she needed to use her ship for more lucrative purposes if she wanted to keep it. After that she began leasing it out to private corporations for various jobs: cargo transfer, security escort, and, most recently, mining operations. The mining gigs were a bit more wear and tear on the ship, but the pay was well worth it. Amai was able to hire Bryn and Tina on full time, and the Company always sent extra hands along, free of charge.

Two hours into their journey, Amai was studying their flight plan and comparing their trajectory to their anticipated coordinates. Bryn was splayed out in her chair, staring at the stars they moved slightly closer to, but never perceptibly so. In two hours, the two hadn't said a single word to each other. Bryn learned quickly that Amai preferred silence while she was working, and since Amai was her captain, she learned to keep quiet.

The only things Bryn talked about were strictly flight related or to announce her comings and goings from the cabin, so Amai knew when she was alone or with company without having to look up from her screen.

"I'm going to make some coffee," Bryn said. She waited a moment to see if Amai would request she bring her a cup as well, but when Amai said nothing, Bryn stood up and made her way to the kitchen.

Bryn had to enter a specific code to move in and out of the cockpit, but the rest of the ship was open access to all of them. She passed the sleeping quarters to see Maverik and Gabe both sprawled out on beds and snoring. Bryn wasn't especially surprised. Just the night before, as Bryn was finishing up her last beer at The Nebula, she saw Maverik and Gabe saunter in, just starting their night at 1AM. Honestly, she suspected that they were still drunk at breakfast, and were probably only sleeping it off now.

She tried to tiptoe past them, but even carefully placed footsteps clanged and echoed in the hollow, metallic hallway. Two steps past the entryway, Bryn abandoned all hope of stealth and just prayed that they were in too deep a sleep to hear her. When Bryn made her way to the kitchen, all the way at the end of the hallway just before the engine room, she found Ezreal and Tina deep in conversation.

"You don't understand," Tina was saying, talking almost more with her hands than her words. "The definition of an economy has changed entirely since those theories were first posited."

"Oh, shove off it," Ezreal said, leaning back and laughing.

"No, listen," Tina said, flaring her nostrils so wide her three nose rings all stood at attention.

"They're trying to run the economy as if we had other economies to interact with—to trade with and boost each other up. But there's only *one* economy now. It calls for a whole new set of principles and a different strategy to keep it afloat."

"Oh yeah? And what's that?"

"Well," Tina said, shifting in her seat. "I'm not an expert—"

"You sure?" Ezreal said, his blonde, sharp hair staying perfectly in place as he leaned forward onto the table. "Cause you sure were talkin' with a lot of confidence for someone who isn't an expert."

"Hey," Tina said, raising her hands up in defense. "I can be an expert at identifying a problem without being an expert at solving it."

"Yeah, yeah," Ezreal said, taking a sip of his coffee. For the first time since Bryn entered the room, his eyes wandered off of Tina and he noticed they weren't alone. "Oh, hey Bryn."

Tina turned around and gave her a smile.

"Anyone want more coffee?" Bryn asked. She always made extra when she brewed a pot because it never went to waste. The only way they all stayed sane while trapped in a metal box was through copious amounts of coffee and sheer force of will.

"Yeah, I'll take some more," Ezreal said, gulping down what was left in his cup.

"Please," Tina echoed, pushing her cup across the table.

Bryn divided the coffee between them and sat down at the table, eager for some interaction after hours of complete silence. She listened to Tina and Ezreal talk about the economy some more before moving on to the new colony being established on Mars. Bryn was surprised to find Tina and Ezreal both agreed that a new colony on the southern end of Mars was a waste of resources, but it was back to business as usual when they began to talk about where those resources should be spent instead. Tina thought that instead of founding a new colony altogether, it would be much more efficient to just expand one of the existing ones; Ezreal argued that we shouldn't be building or expanding on Mars at all—we needed to start colonizing other planets.

Bryn sat silently, enjoying her coffee and the banter, until Tina finally turned to her and asked for her opinion. Bryn shrugged. "I don't know," she said. "I don't follow politics." This, of course, was a lie, but Bryn gave up talking politics five years ago when she'd gotten a black eye and a four inch scar on her right arm just for saying she thought the new president was just a figurehead. Tina and Ezreal were nice—she probably wouldn't walk away with a new scar if she actually shared that she thought the colony would be well worth its cost in the amount of ore they would pull out of the southern hemisphere in the next thirty years. Nevertheless, she kept her mouth shut, mostly out of habit and uncertainty.

Twenty minutes after Bryn finished her coffee, she finally made her way back up to the cockpit. She passed Maverik and Gabe, both in the same positions and sleeping soundly. Bryn's hand was at the keypad when she heard a loud clang behind her—the sound of metal on metal.

Bryn whipped around, her heart suddenly racing. She walked the ten paces back to the sleeping quarters, expecting either Maverik or Gabe to peer out toward her and start laughing hysterically at making her jump, but they were both asleep, as still as they had been a moment ago. Bryn walked the length of the hallway, back to the kitchen, looking for anything that may have fallen or snapped along the walls, but everything looked perfectly fine.

She leaned into the doorway of the kitchen and made eye contact with Ezreal, who was once again talking passionately. "Did you guys hear that?"

Tina turned around in her chair. "What?"

"There was a loud bang. It sounded like something was hit hard, or something snapped."

"Oh," Tina said, letting out a small laugh. "That was just the alternator turning over." She gestured to the engine room with her head and then smiled at Bryn. "It's normal. Don't be so skittish, Michaels."

Bryn rolled her eyes and gave Tina a half-hearted wave before heading back to the cockpit. She paused with her hand in front of the keypad, fighting an uneasy feeling that Tina's assurances were not able to assuage. For some reason, no matter how many ships she flew and how many times she came back safe, Bryn was always a little uncomfortable in space. Unlike some of her crewmates, she hadn't grown up in space, so she wasn't used to the sounds and shifting of spaceships that everyone else seemed to be so comfortable with. To Bryn, every clang was a harbinger of collapse; to the others, it was just background noise, like the chirping of birds or the howl of the wind.

Amai was exactly where she left her: hunched over the monitor. But now she was examining the manifest instead of the flight plan. Bryn settled into her seat and stared forward into the void of space.

"Where's your coffee?" Amai said, not looking up from her screen.

"I finished it in the kitchen."

"Is the crew awake?"

"Ezreal and Tina are. The other two are sleeping."

Amai frowned. "Ezreal should be sleeping. We're set to arrive at Io in seven hours and I want work to begin immediately."

"Tight schedule?" Bryn said, almost automatically.

"Always," Amai answered dryly.

Bryn knew that she was expected to tell Ezreal to get to sleep, but she didn't move. Her body was heavy in her chair, and she began to sweat with the thought of the long walk back to the kitchen. She had been reminded of the tenuousness of a ship in outer space and with every step she felt the panels shift beneath her feet, as if she was on unstable ground.

Amai looked over to Bryn, surprised that she hadn't taken the opportunity to get up and leave again. Bryn was always looking for an excuse to get out of the cockpit and roam the ship; she was a restless person, but she was a great pilot, so Amai didn't mind her wandering around when she wasn't actively working. Amai watched Bryn for a moment: her pilot was biting her fingernails and staring at her shoes, completely unaware that Amai was looking at her. Amai furrowed her brow and activated her comm.

"Ezreal," she said and waited for a reply.

"Aye," Ezreal answered, his voice crackling against static.

"Get some shuteye. You're working a full shift in seven hours."

"Understood," Ezreal responded.

Amai turned off her comm, still watching Bryn, who seemed completely disengaged with reality. She took five breaths and finally said, "Bryn."

"Huh?" Bryn responded, breaking her own loop and making eye contact with Amai.

"You okay?" Amai asked, genuinely concerned.

"Yeah, yeah." Bryn shifted in her seat to her usual position and stared out into space.

Amai pulled up her log on her monitor and added in a note about Bryn. Her pilot had done nothing wrong—nothing against protocol—but her behavior was out of character, and Amai had a habit of noting anything anomalous in the captain's log, just in case.

***

The rest of the journey to Io went smoothly. Tina set about fixing minor things around the ship, including the microwave and the suction in the toilet; the Company men ate a full meal and played a few games of poker; Bryn ran through some docking and course correction simulations. And all of them slept, at least a little, except for Amai. Amai checked their flight plan and compared it to their actual course nearly every half hour. The rest of the crew thought her attention to detail in this regard was borderline insane; the autopilot maintained the course so precisely and reliably that some ships had begun running without a human pilot onboard altogether. But they had never been on a ship where the autopilot had failed. So, no matter how much they teased her or raised their eyebrows or uttered incredulous comments, Amai would always monitor her autopilot.

This particular job was close to their launch point, so Amai was able to stave off the call of sleep until they arrived. It would take the Company men at least a day, maybe two, to mine the amount of platinum they were contracted for, and in that time Amai would get plenty of sleep.

When Bryn returned to the cockpit from her nap, they were just approaching Jupiter. Bryn always loved the look of Jupiter—the colors of the desert swept across the surface like a perfectly cast marble. And then there was Io, which looked more like a round of rotten cheddar cheese. Bryn did appreciate that work on such an ugly, desolate planet meant she had more time to appreciate Jupiter from a reasonable distance.

"Are you ready to take us in?" Amai asked, looking up from her screen.

Bryn buckled into her seat and pulled her control panel into position. "Whenever you give the word, I'm on it."

Arguably, Amai was more skilled at all the tasks she asked Bryn to take on; she had trained as a pilot for eight years on a military freighter before the Persika came to her. But if Bryn didn't do things like docking, landing, and takeoff, then all of them, including Bryn, would wonder why she was there. And Amai didn't want to tell them that Bryn was there not because she couldn't pilot her own ship, but because if for some reason she wasn't able to, she didn't want the rest of them to die.

"By all means, take us in," Amai said, finally looking away from her computer and through the thick glass that stood between her and Io. Amai activated her comm and waited for the faint static to greet her before talking. "Buckle in and prepare for landing. We'll hit atmosphere in four minutes."

Several "Ayes" overlapped in the comm, and Amai leaned back into her own seat and buckled in. Bryn's landing was unceremonious, but it was functional. She used a newer technique that favored speed over fluidity, taking them into the atmosphere at a ninety degree angle and then flattening out and spinning for the final portion of the landing. Amai always felt a bit nauseous, but she kept her reservations to herself; Bryn was extremely sensitive to criticism, and she would rather endure some light nausea than risk losing a perfectly suitable pilot.

"And there we go," Bryn said, a smile on her face.

Amai got on the comm. "Alright, section 4 will be depressurized. Suits on if you enter that part of the ship. Tina, you're good to set up the drill; Ezreal, Gabe, and Maverik will be on once it's ready. Let's be efficient and smart, and get this wrapped up in under 36 hours."

Amai switched off her comm and turned to Bryn. "I'm going to get some rest." She waited for an affirmative nod from her pilot and then went straight to her sleeping quarters. The rest of the crew shared a room full of bunk beds, but Amai had a separate room adjacent to the kitchen. It was small, but it was private, which was all Amai needed it to be.

As soon as she closed the door, Amai's heart rate slowed down. She leaned against the wall and closed her eyes, focusing on her breathing.

*In and out.*

*In and out.*

It was a technique the mechanic on her first flight taught her when he found her huddled in a utility closet, tears coating her face and hardly able to breathe. He sat down with her and asked her to breathe along with him. She watched his big belly rise and fall, and she stuck her stomach out as well, taking in as much air as she could and then releasing it in rhythm with his breaths. Marcelle. He taught her other tricks too. "It helps," was all he said. For a time she had used a lot of his techniques, but over the years Amai had forgotten them or simply found them less effective than controlling her breathing. In fact, it was the only thing that worked anymore.

After washing her face, Amai laid down in her bed and put in some earplugs. The sounds of Tina setting up the drill were already echoing throughout the ship, and it would only get worse when the drill was actually turned on. There had been a time when Amai had closely overseen the operations on the ground; where she helped load the cargo or mine the ore. But then she never slept because she was always in charge—in control—and her anxiety went through the roof. So she gave some of her authority to Bryn, who led very differently from Amai. But over twenty three missions Bryn had kept their crew in line and on time, and so Amai slept without significant reservations.

Sometimes, she even dreamed.

***

Bryn found Tina hanging onto the top of the drill, a wrench in hand. She looked small in her navy spacesuit, especially from a distance. The fabric hugged close to her body to improve maneuverability. Little glints of silver caught the light from the ship and highlighted the functional pockets that lined her arms and legs. Bryn flipped on her comm and spoke directly to Tina.

"Everything alright?"

"Almost," Tina answered. "The arm isn't engaging, so I'm lowering it manually."

"It's broken?" Bryn asked.

Tina laughed. "It's from the Company, so it's ancient. Don't worry; I'll have it working in about fifteen minutes."

"Great," Bryn said before heading back into the ship. But she thought, *That's thirty minutes behind schedule.* She hoped they could make it up in the loading phase. She would even help out to make it all go faster.

Inside the ship the boys were all waiting, already zipped up in their suits and twitchy. "Fifteen minutes," Bryn said, and they all groaned. "I know, but it is what it is. You have time for one last piss or a cup of coffee if you need it."

Bryn headed back to the cockpit, taking off pieces of her suit after she entered into section three. Some people didn't mind the suits; some even found them comfortable. But Bryn only wore hers out of absolute necessity. It was tight and hot, and made her feel the slightest bit claustrophobic. Once in the cockpit, Bryn turned on the rear cameras back on. She didn't watch them the whole time, but it was helpful to know if they were on schedule without having to suit up and go out to check.

After about ten minutes she saw Tina emerge from behind the drill and head back to the ship. There was almost no gravity on Io, so she was tethered to the ship with a reinforced line; with each step she jumped several feet off the surface, only to be pulled back down again by her line.

"All set out here," Tina said over the comm.

Bryn replied, "Great. You're up, boys."

As Tina disappeared into the ship, the three Company men emerged. They each got into position without a word. Ezreal was at the drill's main controls, while Maverik and Gabe both set up near the output. As Ezreal started up the drill, the entire ship shook so strongly that Bryn had to grab onto her monitor to avoid falling to the floor. After a few seconds it evened out, leaving just a slight vibration in its wake, almost imperceptible except for the slight hum of the ship's metal resisting the movement.

Bryn watched Ezreal, Gabe and Maverik work from the safety of her climate-controlled, oxygen-filled cockpit. For hours they worked in a loop: Ezreal drilled into the surface; once he reached depth, he pulled the drill out and Gabe and Maverik disappeared into the hole it had made, three times the width of each of them, along with a sizable dolly; nearly an hour later the two emerged with nearly half a tonne of platinum, which they dumped into a pile beside the ship while Ezreal drilled even deeper into the planet's crust. They were so fluid and organized, Bryn almost thought it looked like a dance.

She watched passively for hours, and only realized she'd fallen asleep in her seat when she was woken up by panicked screams blasting through her comm. The entire ship lurched as Ezreal activated the emergency stop on the drill.

"Gabe! Gabe!" Maverik yelled over and over again as Ezreal whispered, "Oh shit. Jesus. Shit."

Bryn's eyes darted to her monitor, still displaying the rear cameras. Gabe was lying on the ground and Maverik was hunched over him. Bryn shot up and started to put her suit back on. She secured her gloves and her helmet as she ran down the hall and straight into Amai as her captain emerged from her quarters.

"What's going on?" Amai asked, startled at Bryn's pace and expression.

Bryn shook her head. "I think Gabe's injured. I'm going out to check." Bryn didn't wait for Amai's response before she rushed toward the back of the ship. In one swift motion, Bryn grabbed a tether and clipped it into place. The moment the doors opened, she stepped onto the surface of Io and beelined straight for Gabe, but her movement was slow in the low gravity. It took her almost a minute to get to him, at which point Ezreal had arrived at his side as well.

Maverik was grasping Gabe's shoulders and begging him to wake up. Ezreal was trying to read his vitals, but Gabe wasn't moving. "What happened?" Bryn asked, unable to look away from Gabe's pale face.

"He just dropped," Maverik said.

"I don't know," Ezreal added. "But the drill started to read errors right after it happened. Maybe something got dislodged."

Ezreal's words were lost on Maverik, who kept urging his friend to get up, but Bryn's eyes widened as she grasped what he meant. "Let's get him inside," Bryn said, reaching for his feet.

As they made their way back to the ship, Bryn noticed little spheres of red liquid flowing from Gabe's helmet. They floated behind them before slowly falling to the surface, like feathers, and staining the yellow dirt a dark orange. Bryn felt a weight drop in her stomach when she realized she was probably carrying a dead body.

When they reached the ship, Tina and Amai were waiting for them. Section 4 was still depressurized, and there was nowhere to put him in the engine room, so they had to carry him into section 2. As soon as they passed through the door, Gabe sagged in their arms and Bryn found herself glad she had taken his feet. They moved quickly to get Gabe to the kitchen, their feet moving in perfect synchronicity, and laid him out on the same table Bryn had been drinking coffee at only a few hours before.

Bryn removed her helmet and gloves and threw them behind her. She pulled off Gabe's left glove and searched for a pulse on his wrist. When she didn't find one, she turned to Ezreal. "Take off his helmet. We need to start CPR right now." Without missing a beat, Bryn locked eyes with Tina. "Go get the defibrillator, and the whole med kit. I don't know what we need yet."

Bryn's heart was racing. It had been years since she was a MediTech, but she remembered the basic steps. She could feel Amai staring at her. She could hear Maverik sobbing in the corner. But her eyes were focused on Gabe's helmet as Ezreal struggled to remove it.

"It's stuck," he said, his fingers slipping on the plastic. Ezreal looked around the room and grabbed a butter knife from the magnet above the sink. He wedged it in the seal around the neck of the helmet and leveraged it until the plastic cracked and the seal popped open. Blood poured out of Gabe's helmet and onto Ezreal's feet.

The smell of iron filled the room.

Ezreal pulled the helmet fully off of Gabe's head; a small pool of blood remained in the helmet, and more continued to drip from Gabe's skull onto the kitchen floor.

None of them had moved before Tina came running back into the room, supplies in hand to save Gabe's life. But she hadn't stepped more than two feet into the kitchen before she fell to her knees and began to dry heave.

"Well, Bryn," Amai started, taking a deep breath. "How do we proceed?"

Gabe was dead. They could all see he was dead. It would be more than appropriate to simply call a time of death and cover Gabe's lifeless face, but Bryn looked around at all of them—scared, terrified even, not even necessarily that Gabe was dead, but what it meant that he was dead—and she made a selfish call. "It's a head wound, but we don't know how deep. Amai and Ezreal, start CPR and charge the defibrillator. Tina, help me get the scanner calibrated. We shouldn't give up on him until we know he's definitely gone."

They all sprang into action, willing and ready to do what they could. For over an hour they fought to bring Gabe back to life, each one of them so utterly focused on their small role that none of them noticed that when Maverik stopped sobbing, he began to pray.

## Chapter 3 - 5.06.2231
## 06:32, Earthtime

Gabe's time of death was called at 22:48 on May 5th, Earthtime. The scans of his brain revealed an object of nearly an inch in diameter settled just behind the bridge of his nose, which had entered at a 45 degree angle in the back of his head. As Bryn had suspected, they had been carrying a dead body in from the dust on Io, and there was nothing they could have done to bring him back to life.

"It was the right call though," Tina said over breakfast the next morning. She and Bryn were the only ones there, up too early to eat with Ezreal and Maverik and too late to catch Amai. The kitchen table had been cleaned, but neither of them sat at it. They each leaned against the countertop without ever saying a word about it. "I'd want someone to do that if it was me." She paused and pushed her oatmeal around with her spoon before looking back at Bryn. "Fight for me, that is."

Bryn nodded. "Thanks."

"Do we know what it was?" Tina said. "What was in his brain?"

"Not yet." When she called Gabe's time of death, Amai announced that they should all wash up and get some sleep, and they would regroup in the morning. It was an unusual move for Amai, who was so incredibly rigid about staying on schedule that it made Bryn nervous if they were slipping behind at all. But these were unusual circumstances. People died in space, of course, but on exploratory missions or in military conflicts. If you were working for the Company, you were probably doing it because you valued your life. People didn't die mining ore on Io, and yet here they were, with a man dead and a lot of questions.

After Amai had dismissed the rest of them, she called Bryn into her room. "I need you to figure out what killed him," she said.

"Me?"

"Yes, you're the one on this ship with a medical background."

"I was a MediTech, not a medical examiner. And we know what killed him," Bryn said, pointing to her head. "Something lodged itself in his skull."

"But what was it? We need to know before we can start up that drill again or depart for the station. I can't make a decision until I know if Gabe's death was an accident or an attack."

"An attack?"

"Just figure out what it is, Bryn. Use the scans or get inside his skull and dig it out. I need you to do this, not just for me, but for the whole crew."

Bryn clenched her jaw, but she nodded.

"Thank you," Amai said, putting a hand on her shoulder. It didn't have the weight it should have. Amai wanted to comfort her, but she didn't quite know how. "We're in lockdown until you report back. Get some rest. Tackle it in the morning."

Bryn had taken her advice, but now that it was morning and she was eating a bowl of congee, she wished she had done it right then and there. She pushed the rice porridge around in her bowl, no longer hungry. Her eyes were drawn to the spot where Gabe's blood had flowed onto the floor and splattered at least five feet across the tile. She knew if she looked long enough, she would find little specks that Amai had missed, even as thorough as she was.

"Did he have a family? Kids?" Tina asked, her voice somber.

Bryn snapped out of her focus on the floor. "I don't know." Bryn threw her bowl in the sink and walked out of the kitchen without another word to Tina. She knew the longer she waited to identify the thing in Gabe's brain, the harder it would be for her to do it.

They had left Gabe's body on the kitchen table last night. His blood was pooled on the floor and his helmet was lying in the corner. They had left it a murder scene, but woken up to a tidy kitchen, all thanks to Amai. Bryn knew her captain had done it without having to confer with anyone else. Amai was anxious and distant and hard to understand, but she was a leader. The kind of leader who sent her crew to bed after witnessing the death of a crewmate and cleaned up the carnage all by herself, leaving behind nothing but the smell of bleach and a note on Bryn's station that directed her to go to section 4 as soon as she was able.

Section 4 was still depressurized, so it was the logical place to store him. The lack of pressure and the cold would keep Gabe's body from starting to decay; ideal conditions for an autopsy, in fact. Though this would be Bryn's first. She put on her suit, along with some especially thin gloves, and felt more claustrophobic than usual.

Bryn went to section 4 alone, only her own breath and the slight hum of her comm to comfort her. Section 4 was for loading and unloading, so the center of the room was empty where the floor dropped out. Along the edges were nearly a dozen seats. It was where the rest of the crew strapped in during takeoff and landing, and in one of these seats, strapped in like he was ready for another takeoff, was Gabe.

Bryn had the strong urge to move him—to examine him on a table—but she knew that moving him would be foolish. There was nowhere else to strap him in, and without gravity he would simply float around the room. So she left him just where he was and set up her scanner. She hadn't been able to get a clear picture of the object last night, even with Tina's help, but Bryn wanted to try again before she sliced up his face to pull it out. It only seemed respectful.

For nearly an hour Bryn tried to capture the object with the scanner, but no matter what angle she tried, it was indiscernible. She finally shut the scanner down and pulled out the med kit Tina had found last night. It had all sorts of useful things: antiseptic, bandages, and clotting gauze. But the only thing Bryn needed was the surgical knife. It was a little thing, and holding it in her hand Bryn realized that it might not do the job. She had grabbed a larger knife from the kitchen, just in case, but she would only use it as a last resort.

Bryn had been sitting next to Gabe for almost an hour, looking at scans of his brain, but she hadn't looked at his face at all. Now she had to look at him. His face was expressionless, and his eyes were closed. They hadn't been closed last night; they had been wide open, staring at all of them, asking why they hadn't been able to save him. Amai must have closed them. Although out of respect or guilt, Bryn couldn't know.

Gabe's skin was pale, all of the color faded away between the loss of blood and the cold. There were little patches on his face that had just started to freeze. The spots spread out like branches on a nerve, searching to make contact with one another. Bryn had considered Gabe particularly attractive. She had actually considered staying for that drink he offered her the night before they took off. But all the things that made him attractive—his smile, the warmth of his face and affect—had all been torn away.

All of the scans had shown the object just behind Gabe's nose, so Bryn decided to try and extract it through his face, rather than digging around in his skull. She suspected that it wasn't standard procedure, but she also knew it wouldn't be standard for her to stick her fist through the back of his head either. As Bryn made the first cut into the bridge of his nose, she prayed that he didn't have any family.

Bryn spent several minutes trying to angle her surgical knife so she could saw through his nasal bone, but she didn't make much progress. She only succeeded in butchering Gabe's nasal bridge. Bryn was grateful that there was no blood flow.

Bryn pulled out the kitchen knife. She lined it up with her other incisions, but just before she began to slice, the butt of the knife caught her eye; it had a thick handle with a broad base. Bryn turned the knife around and lined it up with her incision point. She pulled her arm back and in one swift motion brought the butt end of the knife down on Gabe's nose. With her suit on, Bryn could not hear the crack of Gabe's nose. There was no sound at all in the depressurized cabin. But Bryn felt the bone give and quietly celebrated.

She had some cartilage to get through, but she was able to use her surgical knife for that task. Bryn cut at Gabe's face, silently apologizing for each unskilled stroke, until she hit something that was neither cartilage nor bone—it was metal. Bryn knew that if she stopped to gather her thoughts, she would either cease altogether or make herself sick. So she didn't hesitate before tossing aside the knife and digging her fingers into Gabe's skull. She didn't look at his face—she couldn't. Instead, Bryn stared at the ceiling as her fingers searched behind Gabe's nose for the metal object. She knew it by its smoothness— more even and sleek than bone.

Bryn anchored her fingers around the object and pulled it out in one swift motion. She held it up to the light, not moving her head at all. It was covered in blood, but even Bryn could recognize it as a bolt. It was about an inch in diameter and deteriorated to the point that half of the threads were worn away completely. Ezreal had been right: something had dislodged itself from the drill, and Gabe had been unlucky enough to be in its path.

Bryn breathed out a sigh of relief as she examined the bolt—it was done. Then she looked down at Gabe's face and vomited into her helmet.

***

Amai wasn't sure how to feel when Bryn brought the bolt to her. Part of her was relieved that they weren't being targeted, but she felt a strong pang of guilt knowing that Gabe's death had been completely preventable.

No one would blame her for the accident; there was no amount of control she could have exerted to prevent it. They couldn't claim negligence on her part. Unfortunately, she was almost certain that they would try and blame Tina, even if there was nothing she could have done to prevent it. The Company absolved itself of blame in every way it could, and she knew they would assert Tina had untightened the bolt at some point in her set up of the drill—of course it wasn't *malicious*, just simply incompetent. They would make the argument all because the money they would owe to Gabe's surviving family would be far greater if their equipment had been improperly maintained than if a crewmember had altered the drill outside of its standard calibration. Amai knew the second they docked, a crew of men would be ready and waiting to take away both the drill and Gabe's body, and Tina would be handed a sealed envelope declaring her part in the untimely death of a crewmember. And since Amai knew all of this would come to pass if she did nothing, she enlisted Tina to assist her in collecting their own evidence.

"It came from the drill? You're sure?" Tina asked Amai, hoping she had heard her wrong. Tina's face had dropped the moment Amai had told her the object in Gabe's head had been a bolt.

"I don't see what else it could have come from." Amai handed it over to Tina, who began examining it. "I talked with Ezreal. He shut the drill off because it was malfunctioning, and he only realized Gabe was injured after he shut it down. It seems almost impossible that the two events are unrelated."

Tina turned the bolt over in her hand. "You're right."

"We're not starting the drill back up while we're out here and risking further injury, but before we leave I want the two of us to do a thorough examination of it."

Tina frowned. "Shouldn't the Company do that? It's their property."

"Which means they'll be looking for a scapegoat." Amai paused as her words washed over Tina. "I don't want it to be you, so we need to document the disrepair of the drill now, before we return."

"Understood." Tina handed the bolt back to Amai. "I guess we'll want to put that somewhere safe."

"I will. Now suit up, there's no point in delaying."

"Yes ma'am." Tina started down the hallway but turned back. "And Captain," she said, waiting until Amai faced her as well. "Thanks for looking out for me."

Amai nodded, but she didn't respond. It was her duty as a captain to protect her crew, and it was also her moral duty to find the truth and make it known. But those were only secondary motivations. What Amai couldn't articulate, or maybe simply wouldn't articulate, is that she genuinely cared about what happened to Tina, and if she could help her, she wanted to.

Outside of the ship, they combed over the drill. It had recently been painted a metallic black, but the paint easily chipped away under Amai's fingers, revealing extensive rusting. Amai recorded the entire examination, and even captured a few images just in case the recording became corrupted.

It took Tina nearly thirty minutes to find where the bolt had dislodged; it was at a joint in the arm of the drill. "Look at this," Tina said, curiously. She ran her fingers over a dozen other bolts, tightly packed in the same location. She took out her wrench and unscrewed one, which was in pristine condition.

Then, she removed another, which was almost as deteriorated as the bolt Bryn pulled out of Gabe's head. Amai examined the bolts in Tina's hand and then looked to her for further explanation.

"There are twice as many bolts here than there should be. An arm of this size should be held in by six, maybe, and carefully positioned so as not to crowd each other."

"Why?" Amai asked, looking at the arm, where bolts were placed so closely together, they almost overlapped.

"It weakens the metal," Tina said, shaking her head. "Instead of replacing the bolts here as they wore down, they just added more in." Tina sighed and looked at Amai. "Probably a bunch of Company workers trying to meet a deadline. Greenhorns who didn't really know what they were doing."

Tina screwed the bolts back in and Amai asked, "What do you think would happen if we turned this back on?" Amai knew they should probably cut their losses and return to the station. She knew, from Tina's explanation and her own examination of the drill, that it wasn't safe to operate anymore. But part of her also knew that the Company would punish her for failing to mine the amount of platinum they'd agreed upon, and so she had to ask.

Tina raised her eyebrows. "I'd guess you'll have a few more bolts fly off, if not into someone's head, then into the ship's hull. And then the arm would fall off, likely while spinning—hard to say what direction that would fly off in. Personally, I wouldn't take my chances."

"Understood," Amai said. "Let's secure the drill and the payload for takeoff. I'll have Ezreal and Maverik come out and help."

Tina gave her a thumbs up and Amai returned to the ship. She headed straight for the cockpit and uploaded her video to the ship's hard drive. She would send a copy of it to the Company, along with the message that they would only be returning with a third of the agreed upon amount of platinum ore and one less member of the crew. But Amai sat for several minutes deciding if she would only send that message to the Company or to the authorities as well.

In the past eighteen months, most of her work had come from the Company; she was efficient, effective, and—to her shame—discreet. On two of her previous jobs, her crew had walked away with injuries; they had been minor, so Amai bent to the Company's will and withheld her reports from the authorities. It was against protocol, but it's also what kept her in the good graces of the Company, which paid double the going rate for her ship and its crew. But those incidents paled in comparison to Gabe's death.

She knew the Company would likely blacklist her if she reported it, but Amai decided the possible consequences for keeping silent were too great: Tina may take the fall. Gabe's family may never be compensated or find closure. Amai might even lose her moral code altogether if she attempted to justify such a choice.

Amai drafted another message with all the same components, but this one she sent to the reporting authority on Ligon Station. As she sent it out, she felt a deep pit form in her stomach. She had done the right thing, but it would come at a cost.

As she sat in her chair, working up the energy to join her crew in loading the cargo, Amai mourned for the future she thought was secure, and that she was sure was gone.

\*\*\*

As the rest of the crew made arrangements outside of the ship to prepare for departure, Bryn sat in the cockpit, running through simulations. Amai asked her to run through takeoff and docking procedures at the new payload dimensions. Bryn had protested at first; she felt her efforts would be better spent helping the rest of the crew outside—the sooner they could leave the better, and it would be good for morale to see her helping.

"And it will be good for morale to get back to Ligon Station without any further issue," Amai had replied, sending Bryn to the cockpit.

Bryn had done more simulations under Amai than she had done in her seven years of piloting before signing on with her. At this point, she could land, dock, and maneuver with her eyes closed. But it was not her ship, and if she wanted to get paid, she needed to follow orders. So Bryn sat in the cockpit, running simulations ad nauseam until Amai told her she could stop.

Every few minutes, Bryn's eyes wandered to the rear cameras. The drill had been easy enough for Tina and Ezreal to secure, but they spent hours adjusting the mesh net that would tow the platinum ore behind the ship. The net was designed to hold nearly ten tonnes of platinum, but they only had about three. If they loaded it without making any adjustments, all of the platinum would shift to the back of the net, away from the ship. This would be fine while they travelled through space, but when they tried to dock at the station it would throw off their center of mass and they risked losing control of the ship. So, they had to find a way to adjust it. Bryn watched as they tried nearly a dozen solutions to shorten the massive net until they finally settled on a simple, but sizable knot halfway down the net, which took all four of them to tie.

They finally set about loading in the platinum and in just under four hours they were back in the ship. Amai gave Tina, Maverik, and Ezreal twenty minutes to use the toilet and get a drink before takeoff, but she went straight to the cockpit.

"How were the simulations?" Amai asked Bryn when she entered the room. Bryn was still staring down at her screen, seemingly engrossed.

Bryn popped up and smiled. "Great. All set?"

"Yes, and the rest of the crew will be ready in twenty. Can you repressurize section 4?"

"Yeah, no problem."

Amai sat in her chair and pulled up the flight plan. They were taking off nearly fifteen hours before their scheduled departure, but the change actually saved them a bit of fuel and a few minutes in flight time because of their orientation to Jupiter. The computer calculated a smooth flight with no interference. Amai breathed out and felt her pulse relax.

"Captain?"

Amai snapped to attention at the sound of Bryn's voice. "Yes?" she said, looking over to her pilot.

"Did you move Gabe's body?"

Amai furrowed her brows. "No."

"So, he's still in section 4, strapped in that seat?"

"Yes."

"Don't you think we should move him?" Bryn said cautiously.

"It's the most logical place for him; he's secure in that seat."

"Yes, but it might upset the crew to have to see him like that. I think we should move him."

Amai knew Bryn was right, but there was no logical place to move him. It hardly seemed appropriate to stuff him into one of the storage cabinets. "Where would you suggest?"

Bryn shook her head. "I don't know, but away from the rest of the crew."

"I don't want to disrespect his body," Amai said.

"The living come first," Bryn said, no hint of irony in her voice.

Bryn offered to help her, but Amai insisted she would do it herself; although she did have Bryn switch off the gravity in most of the ship after giving fair warning to the crew. Amai floated over to Gabe and unbuckled him. She had seen his face after Bryn removed the bolt. When Bryn came to her, covered in her own vomit, Amai knew she couldn't leave him exposed, so she'd returned his helmet to his head and secured the broken plastic with a bit of electrical tape. She realized now, as she was thinking about stuffing his body into a storage cabinet, that taping his helmet back on had been unceremonious as well.

Ultimately, Amai brought Gabe into her own room and strapped him to her bed. She knew that as his body thawed and the gravity was reinstated, some of his blood would seep into her sheets and mattress. The smell of iron and decay may even linger long after they docked at Ligon station. But it was the least she could do, for both her crew and for Gabe.

Amai made her way back to the cockpit and gave the rest of the crew a five minute warning. "We're getting off this fucking moon," she said, her heart racing.

It was the first time Bryn had ever heard her captain swear.

*** 

Bryn had practiced taking off of Io with the new payload size fourteen times in the simulator. In each iteration, her technique was flawless, with a 100% success rate, and in reality she performed no differently. They were off without a hitch, just as Amai had requested. Bryn activated the autopilot as soon as they were clear of Io, and she sat back and watched space pass by in front of her.

Amai cleared the crew to leave section 4 and move about the ship, and she set to pouring over the flight plan and cross checking it with the autopilot's trajectory. It was routine as usual, except for the shadow that hung over them.

They were two hours into flight when Amai spoke to Bryn. "Are you doing okay?"

Bryn was caught off guard. She had been lost in thought, staring off into space. In all her missions with Amai, her captain had never started friendly conversation mid-flight. Sometimes she struggled through a brief talk in the landing bay or responded cordially when asked about herself, but Amai was not one to start an exchange of pleasantries. "Good—I'm good," Bryn stammered.

"Are you truly?" Amai asked, looking up from her screen and sitting straight upright.

Bryn sat for a moment and finally said. "I guess not."

"Me either," Amai said, refusing to break eye contact with Bryn. "Have you ever had a crewmate die before?"

Bryn shook her head. "Injuries, sure, but no deaths."

"What about when you worked as a MediTech?"

"A few," Bryn said. "But it was different. They were strangers; I didn't know them."

They sat in silence for a few seconds before Amai spoke again, "I've seen a lot of death. When I was in the military, I lost a lot of colleagues—a few friends. And my parents…in the Vivaldi failure."

Bryn's eyes widened. The Vivaldi failure was known far and wide as a completely preventable catastrophe; a fable told across the system about greed and overreaching. But Bryn had never met a single person who had been personally affected by it. "Your parents died on the Vivaldi?" Bryn echoed, unsure of what to say. "I'm sorry, that's horrible."

"It was," Amai said, her eyes glazing over as she retreated into her memories. "I was there to see them die." Amai watched Bryn's expression turn from one of sympathy to shock. It was the reason Amai never told anyone she was a survivor of the Vivaldi; there were fewer than a dozen of them and it branded her as broken. A person doesn't witness such horror and come away unscathed—at least that's what her lawyers had argued in the lawsuit that bought her this ship. They were right.

"I'm not looking for sympathy," Amai said, "but I've seen death firsthand—a lot of it—and it doesn't get easier. Gabe's death stings like a knife in my heart. Somehow it might even be worse because I'm the one who was supposed to keep him safe."

"It's not your fault," Bryn said, fully believing her words.

"Knowing that and feeling it are different things. One day, I'll feel okay from Gabe's death. You will too. But it won't leave you. It never does."

Amai clenched her jaw and turned her attention back to the screen. Bryn knew she was done; Amai had said what she intended to say. Bryn didn't know if she felt better or worse, but when she turned her attention back to the window, she didn't slip back into a spiral of thoughts and fears. Instead, she watched the space in front of her, fully focused on what lay ahead of them.

***

Five hours into their flight, an object caught Bryn's eye. She had been staring at clear space in front of them, so even the slightest movement in the periphery stood out as notable. And even more notable was that it was coming toward them.

Bryn moved for the first time in hours, her limbs resisting the movement. She leaned over her screen and scanned for ships in the vicinity, but nothing came back. Bryn looked back up, expecting the object to be gone—some figment of her imagination—but there it was, drawing nearer.

"Anything coming up on your monitor, Captain?" Bryn asked, not taking her eyes off the object that was headed toward them at an alarming speed and looking more and more like a ship.

"No, nothing," Amai responded, hunched over her monitor.

Bryn inched forward in her seat, but the straps across her chest kept her from standing up. With every passing second, the object grew larger, and Bryn became more assured in her assessment. "I think another ship is approaching us."

"What?" Amai didn't look up; she didn't trust the subjectivity of her eyes. She trusted the objectivity of the instruments on her ship—the cold, unfeeling precision of sensors and scanners and circuits. So Amai pulled up the scanners again and examined them, but there was nothing amiss. The space around them was clear. "There isn't another ship within half an AU," Amai said, still staring down at her screen.

Bryn didn't have enough time to correct Amai—to tell her the scanner must be malfunctioning or to just look up and see it with her own eyes. The ship was headed right at them. It was a massive gray freighter, at least three times their size, and Bryn felt in her gut that if she didn't move, it would plow right through them. She grabbed the controls and performed evasive maneuvers. "Hold on!" she screamed, unsure if she had activated her comm or not.

She pulsed the engine and sent them veering off course, but out of the path of the other ship. Then she shut the engines off and activated the stealth mode, enabling them to coast on their current trajectory without releasing a heat signature. Bryn's heart was racing, but when she turned to look at Amai it almost stopped.

"What are you doing?" Amai yelled, pulling herself off the floor. She hadn't been buckled in when Bryn pulled them off course.

"I'm sorry," she said quickly and flicked on her comm, "I'm sorry. Is everyone okay?" One by one they sounded off, reporting bumps and bruises, but otherwise intact.

"There was another ship, coming right for us," she said, pointing in the direction the other ship would now be. "You didn't see it?"

"No, I didn't see it. And neither did the scanners. Are you sure?"

"There was no mistaking it," Bryn said confidently. "Reboot the scanners, they must have malfunctioned."

Amai looked at her skeptically, but she went about manually rebooting the scanner. Her ship wasn't the newest model, but it wasn't old either—certainly not old enough to have fundamental tech malfunctioning. It took nearly five minutes for the scanner to reboot, and Amai counted every second of it as her heart pounded. They were well off their expected trajectory, and she needed to correct it as soon as possible. But if Bryn was right—if there was a hostile ship nearby—then getting back on their reported flight path would be exceedingly unwise.

Amai recalibrated the sensors and set it to scan for both heat signatures and magnetic waves. If something was out there with them, Amai would find it. But there was nothing. Bryn implored her to run it two more times, and Amai obliged, but still the scanners found nothing.

"Captain, I saw it. There's another ship out here. I don't know how it's evading our sensors, but it is."

Amai sighed. "Maybe you should get some rest. We've been under a lot of stress, and you've been up for a while. Your eyes might just be playing tricks on you."

"I know what I saw."

"You know what you *think* you saw," Amai said, trying to balance sternness with sympathy. She could read Bryn's face like a map: her pilot wasn't lying. But that didn't mean she was right either. "Go get some rest, Bryn."

Bryn tried to protest, but Amai would not hear her. "What if the scanners are wrong and there's someone waiting out there for us? Just waiting for us to pull out of stealth and blow us to pieces? You need me here to perform evasive maneuvers."

"Get some rest, Bryn," Amai said more sharply. "That's an order."

Bryn left the cockpit with every muscle in her body under tension. Her captain was so reliant on technology that she was going to get them killed. She stomped through the halls, past the sleeping quarters, all the way to the kitchen to make herself some coffee. She found Tina and Ezreal there again, but this time they weren't arguing fervently about the new announcement to terraform the arctic—they were silent and still, nursing a few bruises and thinking about the death of their crewmate.

Bryn poured her coffee and sipped through nearly half of it before Tina finally spoke to her, "What was that about?"

"What?" Bryn responded, only half engaged. Her mind was still in the cockpit next to Amai. They hadn't changed course yet, so maybe the scanners had picked something up. Bryn simultaneously prayed that she would find something and that she wouldn't. If there truly had been no ship, then they were safe and could resume course. But that also meant that Bryn had hallucinated the whole thing, and that was something she could not stomach. No matter what the scanners said, she knew there was a ship out there lying in wait for them; she would bet her life on it.

Tina looked incredulous. "*What?* The sudden jolt out of our trajectory." She showed Bryn a bruise running down the length of her forearm that had already started turning a deep shade of purple. "I have one to match on my leg. Ezreal almost lost an eye."

Bryn looked at Ezreal and sure enough there was a two inch gash above his left eyebrow that he'd hastily patched up with some clotting gauze and thin strips of surgical tape.

"I'm sorry," Bryn said. "There was another ship—I saw another ship," she emphasized, "coming right toward us. It was going to hit us if I didn't pull us off course. It all happened too fast for any warning."

Ezreal and Tina both perked up with nervous energy. "Another ship?" Ezreal asked.

"A freighter about three times our size," Bryn said, downing the rest of her coffee. She got up to make another cup. "The thing is…the scanners didn't pick it up."

"Some new stealth tech?" Tina offered.

"Could be," Ezreal said. "Or maybe our scanners have been tampered with."

Tina rolled her eyes. "Who would tamper with our scanners? We're just a small merc ship."

Ezreal shrugged. "A small merc ship that just failed to meet its contract and stands to spark a media nightmare for the Company." Bryn and Tina looked at Ezreal with blank faces, so he continued. "Gabe's death—Tina and Amai took all that footage to prove that it was the Company's negligence that caused his death, right? Well, they would stand to benefit from keeping that from reaching the light of day." He paused for a moment before adding, "Amai wouldn't be dense enough to send them all of that before we returned, right?"

Tina and Bryn exchanged glances. They both knew that Amai was not dense, but she was a rule follower, and the Company required ships to report updates and rationale for changes in mission execution and flight plans.

"They know," Tina said. "But would the Company really take us out to cover up Gabe's death? An entire ship? There would be an investigation then too."

Tina and Bryn worked directly for Amai, who was merely contracted out by the Company. Neither of them had actually worked *for* the Company before, so they both looked to Ezreal. He had been with the Company for nearly 5 years.

Ezreal grimaced. "I've seen them cover up some heavy shit before—injuries all the time, but even a few deaths. They pay out what they can and push the blame away from themselves. I've never heard of them taking out a ship though."

"It would be too risky," Tina added. "Are you sure about what you saw?"

"I'm certain," Bryn said. Although each time someone asked her that question, she became a little less sure. Was she overtired? She thought maybe she should get some sleep. Amai had ordered her out of the cockpit and to get some rest; even if she wanted to protest further, she wouldn't have much luck. Amai would send her out of the room as soon as she opened the doors. And even if she could get a word in, Bryn wouldn't be able to change her captain's mind—the only thing Bryn would gain from pushing Amai further is a letter of termination. So Bryn silently prayed that she was wrong—that her eyes had been playing a trick on her and there was no other ship—and she went to get some sleep.

*** 

There were three levels of codes on The Persika: general access, secondary access, and primary access. The entire crew had the general access codes to come and go throughout the ship as needed. Tina and Bryn both had secondary access codes; they could shut off certain parts of the ship or lock down sectors. In the event of an emergency, the ship automatically defaulted to secondary access to maintain order. Amai was the only one with primary access—she could override all of the other codes to lockdown the ship, adjust the gravity, and control life support systems at any time.

The tiered coding system was built into the ship's protocol, but it was expected that more than one individual had the primary access codes. Unfortunately, Amai had never trusted anyone enough to give them full control over her ship, so she alone knew them. It was because of this that she tried to use her primary access privileges as sparingly as possible. If something happened to her—if she had a heart attack or an aneurysm—the ship would be locked in whatever state she'd left it in. It was a risk Amai was uncomfortable with taking. So even though she could have sealed the cockpit door as soon as

Bryn walked through it, she ignored the nagging feeling to lock her pilot out. She had to pray that her order to Bryn to get some sleep was enough.

Amai took her time combing through the ship's data from the previous hours. She looked for any irregularities or discrepancies in the data, but everything aligned perfectly with expectation. She ran further diagnostics on her scanners, but they appeared to be functioning normally. Although Amai had to admit that she did not have a strong background in scanner technology; all she knew was that the code was coming back clean.

"Tina," she said over her comm.

"Aye," Tina responded.

"Can you take a look at some hardware for me? Make sure it's working properly?"

"Sure—what do you need?"

Amai watched Tina through the rear cameras as she emerged from the ship. She was particularly adept at maneuvering in zero gravity, a necessary consequence of being a ship mechanic.

Tina set about checking four different sensors around the ship. For each one, she lifted off a panel and removed the sensor from its protective coating to examine it for physical damage. After confirming it was intact, she plugged a meter into it directly and relayed the readings back to Amai. The final step was to test their functionality with a field test, which in this case meant Tina holding a small heater at a distance of twenty meters and then activating her radio. All four sensors passed this test, accurately and precisely detecting the heat signature and electromagnetic waves Tina was sending toward them.

"That one checks out too," Amai said, as Tina radioed her over the last sensor. "You can head back in."

Amai had done her due diligence. She combed over the data and confirmed that the instruments to measure it had been working properly, which left only one logical explanation: Bryn had been wrong.

Her pilot had been under a lot of stress the last twenty-four hours—they all had. It was not easy witnessing the death of a crewmate, and Amai realized she had asked too much of Bryn. She should have given them more time to process before resuming business as usual. She shouldn't have asked Bryn to perform the autopsy.

Amai realized she'd made a mistake in ordering Bryn to determine Gabe's cause of death when she found Bryn in the hallway, covered in her own vomit. Amai had taken her helmet from her and cleaned it herself; she even dropped an additional week's pay in her account. And then she'd merely hoped that Bryn would recover and rise to the occasion because she had to. It was unfair of her to assume she would be ready for duty so quickly after such an experience.

Amai didn't know much about medicine or the brain, but she knew a lot about trauma. Over the course of her teenage years, every psychologist they sent her to talked about her trauma and how it affected her—how it altered her. And then when she served in the military, Amai saw the effects of it on her friends. She saw how trauma ripped away their sense of comfort and twisted their experience of reality. She watched as they lost a sense of themselves and became someone else just to get through the day. She heard some of them screaming out in the night and running from fabricated enemies, as real to them as the people in front of them.

And even with all of her experience with trauma, Amai had not thought twice about asking Bryn to dig into the skull of her crewmate to find the culprit in his death. She had assumed Bryn's medical background would buffer her against any unpleasantness inherent in such a task, but she had been wrong: she had sent Bryn headfirst into battle without armor. Bryn's trauma was her fault, and Amai felt the guilt of it swell inside of her.

She thought for a while on how to proceed. It seemed unwise to tell Bryn she thought she was hallucinating; people didn't like being told they were wrong, let alone losing their grasp on reality. But she needed to assure the crew that everything was fine before starting up the engines again and moving on. She suspected that Bryn would have stopped by the kitchen or run into some of the crew before heading to the sleeping quarters, and she needed to explain why she had Tina check the sensors. So Amai spent twenty minutes outlining their situation in terms as simplistic and comforting as she could manage. Then, she called a meeting in the kitchen so they could all sit around a table together.

It had been almost four hours since Bryn had pulled the ship off course and shut off the engines, and in that time the crew had grown anxious. She could see it in their movements: Ezreal's legs were restless; he jiggled them under the table and unconsciously tried to use his hands to settle them, without success. Tina had bitten her nails to nubs. And the bags under Bryn and Maverik's eyes had grown even darker. Amai knew it was her job to calm the nerves of her crew, and she was determined to succeed.

"Several hours ago, Bryn performed evasive maneuvers in response to a ship she believed was coming toward us, which she identified visually. This ship was not picked up by our sensors. Since then, we've pulled out of our trajectory and turned off the engines to assess the situation. I've spent several hours evaluating our data and checking the functionality of our sensors. I'm happy to report that our sensors are fully functional, and we were not under threat by another ship. We're going to start our engines back up, return to our previous trajectory, and continue on to Ligon station. Any questions?"

"If it wasn't a ship, then what was it?" Tina asked.

"I'm not sure," Amai said. "I wasn't able to make a visual confirmation, but the sensors did not show an object in our vicinity at that time."

"Could it have been an asteroid or something?" Ezreal asked.

"No, our sensors would have picked it up," Amai said. "Asteroids have very specific heat and electromagnetic signatures."

"Maybe it was nothing," Maverik said, his voice soft and detached. Then he looked at Bryn. "You wouldn't be the first to hallucinate something in space."

Bryn squirmed in her seat. The idea that her mind had conjured the other ship had kept her from getting any sleep the last four hours, even though she recognized that she could use it. Her mind kept racing, with thoughts of whether or not she was going crazy.

"Is it possible someone has compromised the code of our sensors?" Tina asked.

"No," Amai said definitively.

"It's just," Tina started, looking around at her crewmates. "If you told the Company that we're coming back early because of Gabe's death, they might have reason to cover that up."

Amai shook her head. "I've run through the code myself, and everything is standard. It would also be impossible for it to be manipulated; there is no remote access to the ship's code. I've also reported Gabe's death and the circumstances of his death to the authorities at Ligon station; retaliation against our ship would not only be pointless, but would open the Company up to further scandal." Amai paused and breathed in deep. "I understand that theories like this may be exciting, but they are not rooted in logic."

The crew was silent. They looked everywhere except at Bryn. All of them believed she had hallucinated the other ship, and they felt that if they looked her in the eye, she would see their pity and their fear. But Bryn wasn't looking at any of them. She was staring down at her hands, telling herself over and over not to cry.

***

After the meeting, Amai pulled Bryn aside to tell her she was taking her off duty for the remainder of the mission. Her captain talked about getting some sleep, seeing a therapist when they landed in Ligon station, and a lot of things about time. *It'll take some* time *before you feel normal again. You need to take your* time *before returning to work. It takes* time *to process things like this.* But all she managed to communicate to Bryn was that she was off duty and, in all senses, merely a passenger on the ship, enjoying a free ride back to Ligon station.

Bryn figured if she wasn't working, she needed a drink.

As a rule, the ship's kitchens didn't stock alcohol; there was no time for drinking on a mission where you're always supposed to be working. But that didn't mean there wasn't alcohol on the ship. Bryn managed to find it in the first place she looked: Gabe's personal bag. He had a forty-year-old scotch nestled between his toothbrush and a wrinkled white t-shirt. It was half empty, but Bryn suspected it might have been full when they left from Ligon station.

Bryn took a long swig. She savored the sting in her throat and the warmth that spread out through her limbs almost immediately. Usually, she hated the taste of liquor, but now she hardly even noticed it. Bryn had four drinks before it occurred to her that there was something decidedly morbid about drinking a dead man's scotch, but by that time she was inebriated enough to find it funny instead of abhorrent. She laughed to herself and let tears flow freely down her cheeks at the same time.

And then she finally fell asleep. She slept without dreaming, sprawled out in her bed on top of the covers, cuddling with a bottle of scotch.

Bryn slept soundly until she was violently thrown from her bed.

Her body flew across the room and her back slammed against the wall. The bottle she had been cradling slipped from her fingers and exploded next to her, shooting little pieces of glass into her skin and soaking her clothes with the strong smell of whiskey. Bryn was pinned against the wall for nearly twenty seconds, unable to lift even a finger away from the metal under the sheer force. And when the force finally dissipated, she fell to the ground. Bryn's body thudded against the hard floor, surrounded by a chorus of clinking glass and creaking metal.

For a moment Bryn sat stunned, breathing heavily and trying to take in her surroundings. Everything that wasn't bolted in or strapped down was in disarray around the room, which included her. Once Bryn started to take account of her own state of being, she winced. Her back was severely bruised, but she was able to sit up and move, so she didn't think she broke it. And her left side—from her elbow to her temple—was covered with little cuts, where shards of glass from the bottle had embedded themselves in her skin. Some of them she was able to pull out, but others were too small or too deep for her to do anything about.

It wasn't until Bryn tried to stand up that she realized she was still intoxicated. She tried to get up three times, but between her new injuries and her state of inebriation, she slipped back to the ground each time. Bryn had no choice but to stay on the floor and turned on her comm. "Hello? Is anyone there?" Some jumbled static answered her before returning to silence. Bryn realized that she'd been hearing that same sound for the last few minutes, but she hadn't noticed it.

Bryn leaned against the wall, unable to get up and feeling the aching of her body grow as the numbing effect of the alcohol slowly wore off. The static in her ear came in waves; other voices trying desperately to reach each other. She wondered if they could hear each other, or if they were also left with the ambiguity of white noise.

A throbbing pain slowly developed in the back of Bryn's head, and when she reached around to touch her scalp her fingertips came back around covered in bright red blood. The longer she sat, the more tired Bryn became. She wanted to keep her eyes open—she knew she should keep her eyes open, but it was all too much. Bryn let the overwhelming need to sleep take her, and the only thing she dreamt of was static.

## Chapter 4 - 5.07.2231
## 14:00, Earthtime

When Bryn awoke again, she was in the cockpit. As she sat up a thick blanket fell off her shoulders, and she felt the full extent of her injuries through the lens of sobriety. With every movement a sharp pain rippled through her back, and when she was perfectly still it faded to a dull ache. Her head was throbbing, though she wasn't sure if it was because she had hit it or if she was merely hung over. And the skin all along her left arm and the side of her face felt like it was on fire.

Bryn was only just getting accustomed to her pain when her surroundings came into focus. The cockpit was in much better shape than the sleeping quarters had been because there were far fewer moveable objects. Amai kept her cockpit clean and tidy—most things were organized and filed away in the appropriate cabinet. If anything had been tossed around in the chaos, it was probably Bryn's last cup of coffee and the pair of slippers she kept stowed away under her chair.

Everything in the cockpit looked to be in its place and in perfect working order, with the exception of the captain herself. Amai was not hunched over her monitor, checking trajectories or monitoring frequencies. Instead, she was standing in front of the main window, holding her comm in her hand and staring out into space. It was something Bryn had never seen her do in all their missions together. She hardly ever deigned to glance out the window.

"Amai," Bryn said, choking out her name. Her voice was strained, as even the muscles in her neck struggled against the trauma.

Amai turned sharply toward Bryn. She put her comm in her pocket and rushed over to her pilot. "Careful, don't push yourself," she said, kneeling down next to Bryn. She placed a hand on Bryn's shoulder as softly as she could. "You've sustained several injuries. I tried to patch you up," Amai said, her eyes darting to bandages she had hastily applied to Bryn's left side to try and stop the bleeding. She realized after they were already in place that she should have sterilized the wounds first, but by then it was too late. She'd used too many of the bandages, and if she started over there wouldn't be enough.

"Thanks," Bryn said weakly, as she looked Amai up and down. Her captain was sweating.

Anxiety and fear were etched across her face, but otherwise she seemed unscathed. There were no cuts on her face; no broken bones; not even a scrape on her skin. Amai had been strapped into her seat when it had happened—whatever *it* was.

"What happened?" Bryn finally asked. She knew what had happened, but she asked anyway. She needed Amai to say it out loud—to admit she'd been wrong. She wanted to hear her say that there was another ship that attacked them, and it was her fault for sending Bryn away.

But all Amai said was, "I don't know."

Bryn sat staring at Amai, stunned. For a while Amai focused on the ground, and then she stood up and shook her head. "We were back on track, moving toward Ligon station in a clear trajectory when something collided with us."

"Another ship," Bryn interjected, sure of herself.

"Maybe," Amai said, uncertainty splashed across her face. "Or an asteroid. Or—or something else. I don't know. The scanners didn't pick up anything." Amai sighed. "And everything's down now; the life support systems are barely functioning and they're pulling every last watt on this ship. I can't go back through the data or look at the footage now."

"Footage?" Bryn asked, her eyes brightening. Most ships didn't record video footage while en route; it was usually a waste of memory storage and the risk to the tech increased dramatically while in flight—for the cameras to properly capture images, they needed to be outside the protection of the ship's shields. Ships that ran their cameras while in flight usually had to replace them at least once a year, and they weren't cheap. In all of Bryn's flights with Amai, she had never known her to run her cameras while in flight. For her captain, the calculation was clear; the risk was not worth it.

Amai nodded. "I turned them on before we started up again; just in case you were right."

Bryn closed her eyes and breathed in deep. She knew what would be on that footage—and she would be vindicated. But even more relieving was that somewhere, deep down, Amai had not written her off as crazy. Even when all the evidence and logic pointed toward Bryn being wrong, her captain had still had enough respect for her to take an additional precaution. Unfortunately, it had not been enough.

"But now we can't check them," Amai said, "which puts us in a tight position."

"If someone attacked us, sending out a distress signal would let them know there were survivors," Bryn said without missing a beat.

"Yes," Amai said. "And to complicate matters further, I've sent three direct messages to the authorities at Ligon station and haven't heard back."

"When did you send them?" Bryn asked.

"The last one was nearly four hours ago."

"Seven hours?" Bryn asked, her eyes widening. She knew some time had passed, since her body had processed all of the whiskey she'd consumed, but she had no idea how long she'd been out. "Amai, how long ago was the ship hit?"

Amai did not answer immediately. She had counted every minute in her head, waiting for a response—praying for one—but with every passing hour she knew that their time was running out. "Twelve hours ago."

Bryn felt the weight of her words. "It's possible that our receiver is down, right? That the message went out, but we're not receiving?"

"It's possible," Amai said, not particularly hopeful. "But it's unlikely that our output is transmitting and our receiver is damaged; the hardware is located in the same part of the ship."

"So why haven't they answered?"

"The message may not have gone out at all; I can't confirm with the systems down. They might not even know we've been hit."

"Or they're not going to help us."

"They have to," Amai said. "If they receive a distress signal, they are bound by law to engage in rescue protocol."

"So, then they haven't received it," Bryn said. A sharp pain surged through her head, spreading from her spine to her temples, and she winced. Amai returned to her pilot's side with a bottle of water.

Bryn drank in small sips, each one more consuming than the last.

Amai sighed. "Yes, they likely haven't received it, but they should know something is wrong because we were due in nearly four hours ago."

"They'll send someone to look for us, right?"

"It's standard to wait 12 hours to account for normal delays or malfunctions. After that they'll send someone, but they'll be searching along our original route; we're nearly half an AU away from our planned trajectory. I was able to use the thrusters to stop our spinning after the impact, but they failed shortly after that, so we've been moving through space in the wrong direction. And they won't know where we went off course. It might be hard for them to find us with any speed." Amai looked out the window, her face devoid of emotion. "They might never find us."

The thought of death left Amai empty, but it lit a fire underneath Bryn's bruised limbs. "How much time do we have?"

"Right now, our limiting resource is oxygen. There's a leak in section two, so if we keep the sections sealed, we have almost three days left. If we open them, we'll have twenty, maybe twenty-two hours remaining."

Bryn almost laughed. "Why would we open them?"

Amai looked back to Bryn, her grim expression contrasted with Bryn's bemused one. "Because Tina's trapped in section three."

## Chapter 5 - 5.06.2231
## 18:05, Earthtime

Amai was strapped into the captain's chair when they were hit.

She usually sat in the copilot's chair, her unsecured belt hanging from the edges of the seat, as it was easier for her to examine the readings on her monitor if she could lean fully over it. For such examination, she had to be untethered. And with Bryn at the helm, she felt secure in preoccupying herself with things like the manifest, the trajectory, or communications from the Company. But when she sent Bryn out of the cockpit, she knew she had to forgo her typical routine and fly the ship.

She sat in the captain's chair and looked straight ahead. She listened for any signal or sign of aberration that the ship's sensors might cry out, but her eyes were locked on the space ahead of her. Part of her was looking for Bryn's ship, wondering if a speck of dust would manifest into a freighter, coming right for them once again.

But there was nothing. Amai hardly blinked, and still neither her nor the ship's sensors detected the blow that hit the right side of the ship. The impact was so sudden and forceful that Amai would have been thrown clear across the cockpit and impaled on the rotator arm if not for the belt strapped around her waist and across her chest. The belt kept Amai in place as the ship spun uncontrollably at close to 6 G's, but her head and limbs all bent to the force, contorting her body into a crescent shape.

It took all of her concentration and coordination to reach forward to the controls and engage the thrusters to stop the spinning, but Amai acted as quickly as her body would allow. Amai knew she only had tens of seconds before the tension in her muscles led to fatigue so great, she would not be able to command them to act, no matter how much she willed them. Then, within only minutes, she would be unconscious as blood pooled in her hands and feet. And if she ever awoke again, she would be subject to the exact same pressures—there was no slowing down in space—but she would be even less likely to overcome them. Amai knew that if she didn't stop the spinning now, she never would.

So, within twenty seconds of the impact, out of sheer force of will, Amai managed to reach the controls and activate the emergency thrusters to counter the spin and return them to a neutral position. She breathed out a sigh of relief but winced with the movement. Her torso and hips were covered in bruises, and she thought she may have a broken rib or two, but overall, she was intact. She had been lucky enough to be strapped in—Amai felt her stomach drop when she thought of where the rest of the crew may have been throughout the ship.

"Status report, status report," Amai said, over her comm. She waited for a full minute to no response before trying again. "Status report, please respond." Amai spoke into her comms, saying the same thing at one minute intervals for ten minutes straight. With each passing minute, the tension in her forehead grew, and Amai felt her breathing becoming unsteady and erratic. Amai finally unbuckled herself and leaned over the monitor to evaluate the status of the ship, but the system was unresponsive. The ship had entered into emergency protocol, which prioritized life support systems and emergency functions, like the thrusters, but all other systems were offline. Amai couldn't run any diagnostics on the ship.

Amai closed her eyes and breathed in deep. Then she slowly breathed out. And in again. She breathed for an eternity, but this time the breathing didn't work. Her heart raced and a panicked scream creeped up from her stomach to just behind her lips, a single breath away from breaking free.

And then Amai finally heard something over the comm: "Hello?" a weak voice said, breaking through static. "Is anyone there?"

Amai recognized it as Bryn. The suppressed cry burst from her mouth, but it was laced with gratitude instead of fear. Amai closed her eyes as tears began to stream onto her cheeks. She sobbed, holding the comm to her ear. "Bryn, are you okay?" Amai asked, but there was no answer. "Bryn," Amai said, desperation seeping into her tone. "I'm here. I'm here!" she yelled, but all she heard in response was static.

\*\*\*

Amai decided she would leave the cockpit the moment she heard Bryn's voice over the comm, but she didn't know how much it would cost her.

The computer was nonfunctional, with the exception of one essential duty: to reflect the status of life support systems. The air filtration system was fully functional and undamaged by the impact; there would be no concern of $CO_2$ or Nitrogen pockets developing and suffocating them quietly.

The artificial gravity was holding steady, so as long as there was some power remaining in the reserves, it would continue to function; Amai was especially thankful for this—if anyone was severely wounded, they would need gravity for any chance of keeping them alive.

It was immediately clear that their most precious resource would be oxygen. The computer estimated that the ship had nine days of oxygen remaining, but that was nearly a week less than it should have been, which meant the ship had a leak. In order to preserve the remaining oxygen, she sealed the doors with her primary access code and switched the ship's full air circulation protocol to circulate by section. It was not a long-term solution; she would run out of air more quickly in the cockpit than her crewmates would in the other sections, but until she could identify the source of the leak, it was the safest option. She needed to preserve as much oxygen as possible, and once she identified the source of the leak, she could omit that section from circulation permanently.

Amai's spacesuit was in her quarters with Gabe's body, but she knew that it wouldn't be safe to move about the ship without one—not with an unidentified leak. Fortunately, the cockpit was stocked with two extra spacesuits. They were stuffed in the top cabinet nearest the door, and Amai had to stand on her tiptoes in order to reach them. She pulled one out and the fabric crunched under her fingers. It was likely older than she was; the two suits had come with the ship—a courtesy of the previous owner, along with an axe and several fire extinguishers. When she purchased the ship, the suits were already forty years old and clearly never used. Amai had considered that a testament to the reliability of the ship that none of the emergency equipment had ever been touched. It hadn't even crossed her mind to replace it. But now that she held the stiff, flaking fabric in her hand of a spacesuit that had been sitting in a cabinet for half a decade, she realized that it had been a great oversight. She would be lucky if the suit was airtight.

Amai stepped into it with great care. The faded olive-green suit was incredibly loose—built to hold a man twice her size, but it appeared functional. Amai snapped her helmet into place and played with the rudimentary oxygen reader on her wrist. She breathed in deep and watched the hand twitch just a little before moving back to center. At least oxygen never went bad.

When Amai took her first step toward the door, she almost tripped. The thick, stiff fabric bunched up around her legs and fought with itself. Amai had to take exaggerated, wide steps in order to keep herself upright. She felt like she was wearing a hazmat suit, not a spacesuit. Amai made a mental note to purchase a few top of the line suits—at least one in her size—for the cockpit.

Putting her access code into the keypad was almost as challenging as walking. The fingers on her gloves were so thick she thought she could have filled them with carrots. Twice she entered her code incorrectly, and she only managed to open the door by grabbing a pencil and using that to push the buttons. Amai slipped the pencil into her right pocket, praying she would have the dexterity to pull it out again.

The cockpit door opened, and Amai felt a coolness in the air, even through her suit. There was no one in the hallway, but there was debris littering the floor. Some of the panels had fallen off the ceiling and a few of the cabinets had opened, spilling their contents. Amai was careful to step over any objects on the ground; she wasn't sure that she would be able to get up if she fell in the emergency suit.

The sleeping quarters were closest to the cockpit, and Amai hoped that was where Bryn was. She might be in the bathroom as well, but Amai pushed that thought from her mind. There were a lot of jutting fixtures in the bathroom—toilets, sinks, shower knobs. All things that could cause much greater injury if one slammed into them than the things in the sleeping quarters. And Amai wouldn't let herself even think about the kitchen. Instead, she prayed that Bryn had followed her orders and gotten some sleep.

Amai had to punch in her code again. Normally, it was a simple, automatic maneuver when she was in her jumpsuit, or even her own spacesuit, but in the cumbersome emergency suit it required more effort and focus—and a pencil. The action was much easier the second time, and Amai almost smiled when the door opened to her, but the sight of the room kept her lips taught. Two bags and a bedsheet blocked her entrance to the room. They were wedged in the doorframe, so secure it was as if they had been built as part of the door. Amai kicked at them for nearly a minute until one of them finally shifted and the whole mess toppled over into the room.

The emergency lights were on, so only soft glow illuminated the room. Objects were scattered across the floor, but most prominently against the close wall, where the force of the spinning ship had thrown them. Among pillows and sheets and a broken bottle was Bryn. She was slumped against the wall, covered in blood and a brown liquid.

Amai went to her as quickly as the suit would allow and bent down over her.

"Bryn," she whispered as she shook her shoulder. "Bryn, wake up."

Bryn didn't respond, but Amai could tell she was still alive. Her chest heaved up and down with labored breaths, as if she wasn't getting enough oxygen, and fresh blood trickled from the cuts on her face. But despite the signs of life, Bryn's lips were turning blue and she was unresponsive. Amai knew she couldn't leave her there.

Amai reached down and tried to lift Bryn in her arms, but her crewmate was too heavy. In any other situation, she would have cut the gravity and moved Bryn in the comfort of zero Gs. But Bryn was injured—the rest of her crew might be injured too. Cutting the gravity meant that any injuries they had wouldn't drain, and pooling blood meant death, so zero gravity was not an option. Amai thought about finding a dolly or a cart, but the only one they had was the mining dolly in section four, and she wasn't sure that it would even fit through the doors of the ship. But the idea was sound—she needed something she could pull Bryn on, and the answer was all around her: sheets. She grabbed a blanket and pulled Bryn onto it. Amai tried to move her as gently as possible, but she didn't have full range of motion in her suit. She pushed and pulled Bryn by her shoulders and her feet until she was fully centered on the blanket. Amai tied the bottom of the sheet in a knot around Bryn's feet and then another, in a loop, at the top. Amai grabbed hold of the loop and dragged Bryn along the ground behind her.

It was a great effort for Amai, as her lungs, gasping for air, pushed against her bruised ribs and then pulled back in spasm. She shuffled down the hallway, pushing debris out of the way with her feet before pulling Bryn along with her. When she finally arrived at the cockpit door, Amai almost cried.

She pulled Bryn in two feet past the cockpit door before collapsing and taking off her helmet. Amai wheezed from both the physical effort and the injuries to her torso. She shimmied out of her suit and found some water. At first she drank greedily, but with every passing sip she realized that she was using a precious resource. Amai forced herself to stop and focused on her breathing, convinced that she could curb her thirst if she only focused on her breath.

But what made Amai forget her thirst was the sight of Bryn. She returned to her pilot's side and examined her wounds. Little shards of glass were embedded in her upper arm and face on the left side—from a bottle of whiskey if Amai recognized it correctly; though it was but a faint memory, as she hadn't had a drink in nearly a decade. Bryn had already pulled out some of the larger pieces of glass. Those were the cuts that bled the most.

Bryn also had a wound on the back of her head and bruising on her back—probably from when she hit the wall. Although some of her injuries were serious, none of them appeared to be life-threatening. Bryn was unconscious, but she wouldn't bleed out while Amai went to look for the others.

Amai wrapped Bryn tightly in the blanket and got in her suit again, but before she put on the helmet, she activated her comm again. "Status report, please respond," she said. Amai waited for nearly a minute before adding, "If you can hear me, I'm coming to find you."

Amai left Bryn in the cockpit and entered section two again. She shuffled down the hallway and was relieved to find that no one was in the bathroom. Amai thought of the bruises on Bryn's back just from hitting the wall in the sleeping quarters. On the same wall in the bathroom were two sinks, which rose to the height of Amai's middle back. Bryn was maybe two inches taller than Amai—if she'd been in the bathroom when they were hit, her back would have broken in half.

Amai breathed in.

She breathed out.

Amai's room was immediately next to the crew's bathroom. She hadn't planned on going back in for the rest of the journey, but she knew that she would make faster progress and be better able to help her crew if she was in her own suit. Amai opened her door and was met with a similar disarray to the crew's sleeping quarters, with the exception of her bed. The bed was still perfectly made, since the weight of Gabe's body strapped onto it had kept everything in place. Amai couldn't help but look at Gabe, but she couldn't see his face through the helmet—some old blood had swirled around inside of it with the spinning of the ship, like a painting done with marbles.

Amai was reluctantly grateful that she was spared Gabe's accusatory gaze. She had already failed him. How many of the others had she failed as well? Amai tried to push the thought from her mind, reassuring herself that she still had two and a half sections to explore where she could both find and rescue her crew.

She stripped off her suit and the full strength of the cold hit her skin. The cockpit had not been nearly this cold; in fact, she had been sweating when she took off her suit there. Either the section's heating element had malfunctioned—which was entirely possible; Amai had cut off the support systems in each section from the others—or the leak was in section two. Amai prayed it was the former. Otherwise, with each trip to and from the cockpit, she was wasting oxygen.

When Amai finally got her suit on and secured, she was shivering. She sealed the helmet and the suit began to warm up her body, but her lips still quivered as she entered into the hall. She was much nimbler and more comfortable in her own suit than the emergency one. Instead of shuffling and waddling through the hallway, she leapt over objects with confidence and moved quickly toward the kitchen.

Her heart raced as she approached the door frame. The door was open, but it was on the opposite side of the hall from the other rooms, so nothing had spilled out into the hallway or blocked the doorway.

The lights in the room were flickering. Instead of emanating a soft yellow, as they were intended to, they overloaded and shorted every few seconds. The room was illuminated with a bright white light, and then bathed in darkness, so Amai had to take in the scene in pieces. It was disarray, as everywhere else, but there were more moving pieces in a kitchen. Doors had opened and spilled out pots and pans and broken dishes. And among them, in the corner nearest the kitchen table, was Ezreal's limp body.

Amai closed her eyes, but all she saw on the black lids was Ezreal. He had to have been sitting at the kitchen table when it happened. His body would have hit the cabinets under the sink, as his head continued forward onto the countertop. His neck would have snapped instantly.

Ezreal's skin was a pale white. Amai could see his head hanging limply off his shoulders, as his eyes stared at the floor, glossy and vacant. It was no use for her to try and save him—he was already gone.

Amai braced herself against the door frame. Her legs felt weak and, despite the bitter cold, sweat began to bead on her temples.

*Breathe in. Breathe out.*

Amai controlled her breathing, but the intrusive thoughts still came like an onslaught breaking through her poorly made defenses. Gabe was dead because of her. Ezreal was dead because of her. How many more of them would she find, lying still against the walls of her ship? How many more of her crew would be dead because she was in charge? Because she hadn't done enough to keep them safe?

Amai was paralyzed against the wall, caught between the realization that she may not be able to carry the weight of another crewmember's death and the fact that if she did not push through, she may be condemning more of them to die. Fifty-four breaths in, and Amai decided that it was not a choice at all—it was never a choice.

She willed her legs to move, and they obeyed, stiff as they were. Amai walked to the end of the hall to the door leading to section three: engineering. It was a section that Amai had walked through a thousand times—one massive room filled with a hundred moving pieces, none of which Amai could identify or explain. The first thing she'd done when she bought the Persika was walk through the ship and examine every nook and cranny to ensure she knew her vessel inside and out. The second thing she'd done was acknowledge that everything in the engine room was completely foreign to her and she hired an engineer. When she first started, and she was dirt poor, she could only afford to hire Tina part time. Tina would check the ship in between runs to make sure everything was running smoothly, like a car mechanic. But once she started running full time for the Company, she brought Tina on full time as well and Amai wondered how she had ever run the ship without her. Tina was always running around fixing things and making improvements—she was easily the busiest person on the ship. And it wasn't until Tina was there all the time that Amai realized how anxious she had been without her. All those missions they'd been naked in the expanse of space, but Tina brought with her not only clothes but a bullet proof vest. At least, that's how it felt to Amai.

Amai was sure she'd find Tina in the engineering room. If she hadn't been drinking a cup of coffee with Ezreal or sleeping with Bryn, she would have been working. There were places in engineering that could have been safe; where Tina would have walked away like Bryn with a few cuts and bruises, but no major injuries. And there were other places where her fate could have been worse than Ezreal's—where her back could have been wrapped around a pipe or her skin blistered and charred on the engine core. Amai tried to push the thoughts from her mind as she entered the vast room, but as usual, they refused to leave.

The emergency lights were not functioning at all in section three, but a red glow emanated from the engine core that illuminated the great, jutting machines that were stationed around the room and cast everything else in shadow. Amai tried to survey the area, as she had with the sleeping quarters and the kitchen, but her eyes couldn't see more than ten meters in front of her. She began to move about the room, starting with the right side, where anything not bolted down would have likely ended up.

Fortunately, there were not many moving parts in the engine room. A bag of loose tools and a few shattered coffee cups were scattered along the wall, but Tina was not among them. The wall was usually alight with buttons and readings, but it was dark. Amai wished she knew how important those things were.

She continued to survey the room, moving between machines that usually sang with life and purpose, but were eerily silent. Amai was three quarters of the way through the left side of the room when she found her mechanic. Tina was not slumped against the floor or impaled on an object, but she was nearly ten centimeters off the ground, pinned under some warped pipes. And she wasn't moving.

Amai took off her helmet and placed it at her feet and then she took off the top half of her suit to release her hands. She was relieved to find that the engine room was like the cockpit—warm and still circulating air. Amai held two fingers to Tina's throat and weakly smiled when she felt a pulse. "Tina," Amai said, shaking her shoulder. "Tina," she said again, more assertively. "I need you to wake up."

Tina's eyelids fluttered and then opened wide as a great scream escaped her lips. She focused in on Amai's face, as her own contorted in pain. Tina started to say something, but her breaths became labored, and she once again slipped into unconsciousness.

"Shit," Amai said, pulling her suit back up as quickly as she could. There was a med kit back in section two that had some sedatives and painkillers. She cursed herself for not thinking about bringing it with her as she moved about the ship.

Amai rushed back to the door. Her fingers shook as she punched in the code, but she managed to open it on the first try. A rush of cold air greeted her as she crossed the threshold. *Was section two getting colder?* Amai didn't have time to assess. She rushed down the hall to the hatch across from the sleeping quarters that held the medical kit. Amai pulled down, but the hatch didn't open. She pulled again, but the mechanism was jammed. Amai punched the handle three times and tried again, but still nothing happened.

Amai didn't care what had shifted or broken during the impact—she was getting in that hatch. She grabbed the handle and jumped off the ground, before reversing the motion and using all of her body weight to pull down on the handle.

Something cracked, and the hatch sprang open, spilling all its contents onto the floor. Amai hardly cared—the floor was covered in all sorts of items and debris. She didn't even notice what came out of the hatch except for the medical kit. She grabbed it and ran back down the hall, almost tripping twice in her haste.

Her hands were steady as she entered the code to section three.

Tina was still unconscious when Amai returned to her side. Amai leaned over the kit, examining the vials nearly an inch from her nose in order to see their labels in the dim, red glow. She picked up each vial carefully, but returned them to the kit carelessly when she realized they were of no use to her. *Epinephrine, Pyridoxine, Amoxicillin*—dozens of medications for different circumstances. Amai had run through nearly fifteen vials before she found what she was looking for: *Morphine*.

Amai unsheathed a syringe and filled it with the max dose: 5 mg. She grabbed Tina's wrist and searched for a vein. Tina's skin was pale enough that her blue veins stood out against her skin. Amai carefully inserted the needle just below her skin and pulled the plunger back toward herself, just as she'd seen medics do on other ships when there was no time for a traditional IV. A small plume of red shot into the syringe and swirled in with the morphine. Amai pushed the syringe down and watched the fluid disappear into Tina's arm. She removed the needle and applied pressure on Tina's wrist with a small piece of gauze.

She waited five minutes, counting the seconds out carefully, before trying to wake Tina again. Amai wanted to make sure she wouldn't pass out from the pain again before trying to wake her up, but she was acutely aware that time was a resource she couldn't afford to waste. She needed to get Tina out of the engineering room and back to the cockpit with Bryn so she could look for Maverik and identify the source of the leak. Every minute, their oxygen store was depleting.

Amai touched Tina's shoulder again and said her name. "Tina," she said. "Tina, wake up."

Tina's eyes fluttered open again, but they maintained a softness as she opened them. As she focused on Amai, her eyebrows furrowed. "Amai?" she asked, a half-smile creeping across her face.

"Yes, Tina, it's me."

"What are you doing here?" Tina asked, her voice distant and calm.

"We've been in an accident, Tina," Amai answered. "I need to get you out of here and up to the cockpit. Can you tell me what hurts?"

Tina looked up and thought for a moment. "My back," she said softly. "And...and I can't feel my legs."

Amai tried to control her expression, but a flash of fear spread over her face. Fortunately, Tina wasn't looking at her; she was still looking at the ceiling. "Tina, can you try and move your right foot for me? Just wiggle it a bit."

"Sure," Tina said. But her foot didn't move.

Amai breathed in deep. Her mind was screaming—crying out—but her face was blank. The next step was to get Tina out of her confinement. Later she could worry about her friend's unresponsive legs or terrifying agony. For now, there was only the next step. That was all she could do.

"I'm going to get you out of here, Tina. Okay? But I need you to tell me if anything hurts as I go."

"Okay," Tina said, returning her gaze to Amai. She smiled at her.

Tina was pinned against some sort of electrical panel. There were several stationed throughout the engine room, but this one was square between a large tank and a group of pipes. Tina's left shoulder was tightly pinned against the tank, which Amai had been relieved to find was room temperature. On Tina's right shoulder and across her chest were two pipes that had dislodged themselves from the others and were pinning Tina to the electrical panel. They were thick steel, but Amai thought she would be able to remove them so long as she could pull them back at the same angle they had fallen from.

The one directly across Tina's chest was only about 10 cm in width. To Amai, it looked like it had buckled under stress and detached from its ceiling attachment, and then swiveled to pin Tina to the electrical panel. Amai decided to pull it straight toward herself with the slightest amount of upward force.

"Okay, Tina," Amai said, planting her feet in a wide stance on the floor and grabbing the pipe shoulder width apart. "I'm going to get this pipe off of you first. Let me know if anything hurts."

The pipe was much easier to move than Amai expected. With a small amount of effort, it began pulling away from Tina's body and Amai thought that getting Tina to the cockpit wouldn't be too difficult at all, but Tina's screams ripped through her thoughts and Amai stopped instinctively.

Tina's cries were sharp and full of agony, as if Amai had just stabbed her through the chest. But Tina was on 5 mg of morphine—she shouldn't have been able to be in so much pain.

"What is it? What hurts?" Amai yelled over Tina's cries.

Tina couldn't answer her. Tears were streaming down her face and her intelligible wails filled the room.

Amai didn't know what to do. She considered ripping the bar back from Tina and trying to pry her off the electrical panel, but she wasn't even sure she could. The pipe on her right side looked like it was pinning her to the tank as well. And she didn't know what kind of damage she was doing to her. The right doctor, with the right tools, could bring feeling back into her legs and eliminate her pain forever—but not if she was dead. Not if Amai pulled her off the panel only for her to bleed to death.

So Amai returned the bar to its original position in front of Tina's chest. Tina's screams quieted and a small whimpering replaced them.

"I'm sorry, Tina. I'm so sorry."

And then there was silence. Tina's head lolled onto her chest and Amai turned away from her. She brought her hands to the side of her head and pulled at her skin, wiping away sweat and dirt and blood, but feeling no cleaner with each pass.

Amai turned back to Tina. She couldn't remove her unless she knew exactly what she was up against. Amai tried to get a better angle from the side, but the forest of pipes was too thick to look through. She tried climbing on the tank and some of the pipes to get a view from above, but each time she slipped off, her hands perspired a bit more and each climb was less fruitful than the last. There was no way to get eyes on the problem, so Amai used her hands.

She breathed out before approaching Tina and putting her arms around her. She felt around Tina's head and neck—both completely unharmed from the sleek metal behind them. Then she made her way down Tina's back. Her hands became slick with blood as little cuts and gashes from dials and buttons peppered Tina's middle back, but they were only flesh wounds. She could stitch those up no problem—they might even heal on their own.

Amai breathed in quickly when she reached Tina's lower back. Just above her tailbone, right in the middle, was a lever from the electrical panel that was firmly lodged in Tina's back.

Amai pulled back away from Tina. She looked down at her fingers, which were capped with Tina's dark, warm blood. There wasn't much blood overall—there was only a small pool of it right below Tina's feet; not even enough to fill a glass with. The lever was buried in her back, but it was also working as a plug to keep her from bleeding out.

Tina's agonizing screams now made more sense. She was hanging several centimeters off the ground, held up by a lever and a couple of pipes. The pipes were actually keeping some of her weight off of the lever, so when Amai tried to remove one, all the weight shifted to the center of her back. 5 mg of morphine never stood a chance.

It was clear that Amai couldn't move Tina on her own. She needed someone to stabilize Tina while she removed the pipes. She needed someone to help stop the bleeding.

She needed someone to help her.

"Bryn," Amai said into her comm. "Bryn, are you awake?" There was no response.

There was one more person who could help her: Maverik. Amai put her helmet back on and made her way to the doors to section four. There was only one airlock between sections on the ship, and it was between sections three and four. Section four was primarily used for cargo storage, so it was often completely depressurized while on site for a mission. To keep section three from depressurizing every time someone stepped out to work on Io or a comet, the ship had two airlocks—one between sections three and four, and another between section four and the nothingness of space. Amai had considered it a luxury when she first bought the ship to have two airlocks. It seemed very cautious. But most of the newer ships had airlocks between every section, just in case. Now, her ship would be considered a safety hazard by most larger operations.

Amai stepped into the airlock, no larger than her bathroom, and closed off section three. She did not depressurize before opening section four—why would she? Section four should have been pressurized, along with the rest of the ship. So, when Amai opened the airlock, she was thrust forward, as if she had been pushed, into what should have been section four.

Her reflexes were quick, so Amai managed to grab hold of the door frame as the air rushed out of the airlock. After a few seconds, the pressure dissipated, and she floated weightlessly next to the door of section four. Without the airlock, all the air within section three would have rushed out along with Amai, and her finger strength would not have been enough to keep her from tumbling off into space as Tina suffocated slowly. Amai had never been more grateful for that airlock.

Amai kept her grip on the doorframe, but she turned around to face section four. Where there should have been a large room filled with cargo and lined with seats around the outside, there was nothing. Amai stared out into the emptiness of space—a million stars staring her right in the face.

Fragments remained that hinted at the former existence of the section of her ship—two feet of floor and arm length pieces of the metal frame jutted out from the wall that she clung to. A single seat remained on the left side of the room, but the rest of them had been torn clean off and were now drifting off in space, probably thousands of kilometers from their current location. And somewhere amongst the debris of her broken ship was Maverik.

Had he died instantly or suffocated slowly in cold silence?

Amai hoped it was quick. She would rather die in an instant than know that she was dying and not be able to do anything about it.

Part of Amai wanted to turn around, right back into the airlock, and return to the safety of her ship—the part that was intact, at least. But another part of her could not look away. Section four was easily the largest part of the ship, making up about a third of its total mass, and it was completely gone. Whatever had hit them had torn clean through her shields and steel enforced supports, something she would have thought was impossible if she wasn't seeing it herself. Any standard asteroid would have left a big dent—maybe even breached the hull—but it couldn't tear through her ship like this. And there were no scorch marks on the metal, so they hadn't been attacked with lasers or rockets or any current weapons tech. But another ship couldn't do this either—the force exerted by a freighter would have torn apart the whole ship, not just a single section. There was no simulation or report or even anecdote that could have prepared Amai for what she saw with her very eyes. Her ship had been deprived of its fourth section and payload—cut clean off from the rest of the ship—and sent into a spiral that knocked them half an AU off course, and she had no inkling of what had incited the incident.

*Breathe in.*

*Breathe out.*

Amai had intended to tether herself to the ship and examine the outside to assess the damage and find the source of the leak, but the tether had been on the far side of the room, so it was gone. Amai wondered if she could find a long rope somewhere, but that seemed unnecessary. The source of the leak was clear, and she would be able to permanently shut off section four while enabling full air circulation between sections one to three. Furthermore, the only person who could help her with Tina was now laying on the floor of the cockpit—maybe she would be able to rouse Bryn from her sleep.

Amai checked on Tina as she went through section three, but her crewmate was still unconscious. She moved swiftly through section two and up to the cockpit, her hands now familiar with entering her code at every door.

Bryn was still wrapped tightly in her blanket, but she had started snoring lightly. Amai went right to the controls and manually shut off the circulation within section four and sealed it. But before linking sections one through three again, Amai checked the oxygen levels.

Amai's heart seized in her chest. "How?" she whispered to herself, leaning over the screen. When she had originally sealed off the sections, there were nine days—almost 220 hours of oxygen remaining on the ship. Now, only a few hours later, that number had dropped by over two thirds. Less than 4 days— 70 hours.

Amai knew it would be less; she'd expected to lose eight, maybe even ten hours while moving about the ship. While she was outside of the cockpit for nearly three hours, there would have been some transfer between the sections, of course. Some oxygen would have been sacrificed. But if the leak was contained to section four, then the loss should have been limited to the air within the airlock—no larger than the size of her bathroom. It was not 150 hours' worth of oxygen.

The answer came to Amai as if she had known it all along but had been denying herself access to the truth. Just the thought of the bitter cold of section two raised goosebumps on her skin and sent a shiver down her spine.

There were two leaks.

And one of them she had been walking through, up and down, for hours, opening sections one to two and two to three, and mingling their air together—diluting their oxygen.

Amai was staring at the numbers on the screen, still partly in disbelief, when she heard static in her comm.

"Amai," the voice said, weak, yet calm. "Are you there, Amai? Where did you go?" Tina's voice cracked and a great sigh gave way to silence.

Amai fumbled with the earpiece, her fingers barely able to grab the silicone, and ripped it out of her ear. She held it tightly in her hand and pushed herself away from the monitor.

Amai stood in front of the window of the cockpit, staring out into nothingness. Tears blurred her vision, but she didn't blink them away. She let the stars in front of her combine and soften, until she saw only light and dark, all at once.

*Breathe in.*
*Breathe out.*

*Breathe in.*
*Breathe out.*

## Chapter 6 - 5.07.2231
## 17:56, Earthtime

Amai stripped off the bandages on Bryn's arm one at
a time. The bleeding had mostly stopped, but it began
anew as Amai used a pair of tweezers to remove the
small shards of glass still embedded in Bryn's skin.
The whiskey bottle had been a dark shade of green, so
the pieces were easy enough to see as long as they
weren't too deep or there wasn't too much blood. But
for every two pieces Amai managed to remove, there
was at least one that she only pushed further into
Bryn's arm, out of sight behind tissue and blood.
Bryn clenched her jaw and ground her teeth the
whole time, but she never made a sound. At the end,
she thanked Amai, even as her cuts wept from the
stinging antibiotic and the shards of glass that Amai
couldn't exhume from her body.

They both sat on the floor. Bryn still hadn't
moved from her spot on the blanket, where Amai had

placed her hours before. Amai sat down and leaned against the cold metal of the wall, her knees pointed to the ceiling and arms resting on top of them. They both breathed heavily and waited for the other one to talk.

Amai broke the silence. "How's your back feeling now? That anesthetic should be kicking in, right?"

Bryn was facing the door. She looked at Amai through the corner of her eye without moving her head. "It's working a little, but I still don't think I can stand."

"What if I try to help you up? Maybe walking around will help stretch it out or something."

Bryn shook her head. "No, I need to rest it."

Amai stared at Bryn. She wanted to insist—to tell her that it was an order. But ultimately, she wasn't even sure rushing out to get Tina was the right thing to do. When Amai told Bryn about their situation, Bryn had steeled up. Her face hardened and she'd turned away from Amai, retreating into her mind to run her own calculations. And Amai let her have that time; after all, she'd had hours to evaluate and analyze their predicament. It was only fair to allow Bryn to have time to process as well. And maybe her pilot would have an alternative—a solution Amai had been too blind and shaken to come up with. So, she gave Bryn some time; a precious resource, but a necessary one.

Amai stood up and went to the monitor. She checked for messages, but there was nothing. She had sent two messages already: an incident ping immediately after the impact and a voice message when she had returned to the cockpit after discovering section four was completely destroyed. The incident ping should have been enough to garner a response—it contained their coordinates and a distress signal, along with any available status reports. A ship should have been on its way less than thirty minutes after Amai sent that ping. But if that was the case, she would have received a ping back.

When Amai returned to the cockpit to find nothing, she sent a direct message to the authorities at Ligon station explaining their situation and directly calling for assistance. That call had also gone unanswered, as had her next four attempts at contact. Amai thought it was time for another message.

Amai decided to record this message with video. Audio was more reliable—less corruptible—but if her first message didn't make it, then there was no reason to expect that a second one would. Video messages transmitted on a different channel than pings or audio messages; maybe this one would get through.

The screen flickered on and Amai saw herself reflected back. She only ever looked in a mirror to ensure there were no large aberrations in her appearance, like grease on her forehead or toothpaste in the corners of her mouth, so looking at her reflection was already a strange experience. But it was made even more disorienting by the fact that she could hardly recognize the person staring back at her. Amai's curly, frizzy hair escaped her bun in every direction, shooting out like lightning bolts around the crown of her head. Her dark brown skin was stained darker with blood along her temples and down her cheeks—blood that wasn't even hers. And lines had started to form around her mouth and under her eyes, making her look nearly ten years older than she actually was.

Amai desperately wanted to change what she saw. She wanted to wipe the blood from her skin and tame her hair, but she knew that would be the wrong call. She needed to fully communicate what had happened to them, and that started with her and the truth inherent in her appearance.

Amai started the transmission and spoke in an official tone. It was a tone that she had learned by listening over the shoulders of her superiors for years and practicing in her bunk at night. Despite all her practice, a desperation lined her words that no amount of training could have prevented. Amai's emotions were well controlled, but they were not conquered.

"This is Captain Amai Menari of The Persika. Approximately twenty-four hours ago we were struck by an unidentified object, which has left the ship severely damaged and inoperable. Several crew members' lives have already been lost. Three of us remain alive. Life support systems are maintained, but we have between thirty to ninety hours of oxygen left. We need emergency assistance immediately. Our coordinates are attached to this transmission."

Amai ended the transmission. She grabbed the water she had been nursing for the last several hours and poured a capful onto a cloth. Amai wiped her face with the cloth carefully, watching the white turn to a shade of crimson as the dried blood slowly dissolved. Then, she pulled the elastic out of her hair. Instead of pulling it back again and fighting with the strands, she let it sit naturally as an afro. Without having to look in a mirror, Amai knew she looked more like herself again.

"Another transmission to Ligon?" Bryn asked.

"Yes," Amai responded, turning around in the captain's chair to face her.

"When do we think about sending a general distress call?"

"I'm not sure. I guess when it's clear no one from Ligon is coming to help us."

Bryn shook her head. "I think that's already pretty clear."

Amai fingered the bloody cloth in her hands, folding it in smaller and smaller squares. "I think we need to decide how likely it is that this was an attack, and then we can make a decision."

"You know what I think," Bryn said.

"You said you saw a freighter coming at us. There's no way a freighter did that. It would have taken out our whole ship, not just a single section."

Bryn laughed and then stopped herself as the motion sent waves of pain throughout her bruised back. "You thought it would be the same ship?"

"What?" Amai said, "Yes, of course."

"That would be idiotic."

Amai furrowed her brow, completely lost.

Bryn stared at her, a confused look on her face as well. She couldn't believe Amai—her captain; the smartest person she had ever met—didn't see what she saw. "If someone was stalking us for our cargo, then, yeah, it would be the same ship. But if someone, like the Company, wanted us taken out, then they would want it to look like an accident. They'd get a ship that's on a similar trajectory to ours and change their course just enough to intercept us. It's textbook."

"Textbook?" Amai asked, skeptical.

"Well, at least in theory."

"You don't understand, Bryn. There's no ship I've ever seen that could tear through us with that kind of precision and not take significant damage itself. If another ship hit us, they wouldn't have walked away from that."

"Yeah, they might not have." Bryn was dead serious, but Amai shook her head.

"No, there's no way. The Company wouldn't do something like that."

Bryn raised her eyebrows. "They wouldn't?"

Amai closed her eyes tightly, her whole face contorting. Even when she opened them again, the muscles were tight around her eyes. "You think this is some kind of conspiracy—that someone is out to get us—"

"The Company is out to get us," Bryn interrupted.

"The *Company* has everything to lose by attacking us." Amai shook her head.

"Gabe's death would cost them a lot."

Amai raised her foot to the chair and leaned over her knee. "What do you think Gabe's death would cost them?"

"Money—a lot of money—to pay out Gabe's family. It would be all over the news; stocks would go down. Regulators might get involved. It'd be a nightmare for them."

"It should be a nightmare for them," Amai said. "But it isn't. Even if they assumed full responsibility for Gabe's death, the payout would be pennies to them. The payload we were hauling behind us was worth ten times what they would have paid in bereavement, at least.

"Regulators would definitely get involved, but they can be paid off too, for two or three times the price of what they would have sent Gabe's family.

The state of the drill they gave us—the reason we're even in this situation to begin with—made it clear that they're already in bed with the regulators.

"And as for the media, well, they usually come pretty cheap. There are so many scandals to choose from that pushing one small incident from the Company where a 30-something nobody died under suspicious circumstances would come at a very small price. That is if they would ever consider running it at all; I suspect not. One death is nothing when people are dying in droves in South America or on the Northern Belt."

Bryn began to look pained, as lines formed on her forehead and around her mouth, but Amai kept going. "So, for half the price of the platinum we were bringing back to Ligon Station, the Company could have wrapped up Gabe's death, no worse for wear. The Company has nothing to lose by taking the fall from Gabe's death. But attacking one of their own contracted ships to cover up a worker's death? If they were caught doing that, then no amount of money could save them. Attacking *us* would be the nightmare: it could cost them everything."

"So, if it wasn't the Company, why don't you send out a mayday call?"

Amai relaxed her expression, which had hardened as she spoke. "Just because the Company didn't attack us, doesn't mean someone else didn't. That payload, even at ⅓ capacity, is worth a lot."

Bryn picked at her cuticles as they sat in a pensive silence. She drank a few sips of water and realized her back was feeling much better; in fact, she hardly felt any pain at all. She began to move her muscles, contracting and relaxing them, and even began to stretch out her spine before she noticed that Amai was watching her. She slowly returned to a hunched posture and took a sip of water. Bryn knew the moment she told Amai her back was okay, her captain would want her to walk—she'd want to open the cockpit door and reduce their oxygen by over half. And Bryn wasn't ready to make that sacrifice, not without some reassurance.

"I think you should send out a mayday call right now," Bryn said, abandoning her cuticles and tightly lacing her fingers together.

"I've only just sent the last call twenty minutes ago," Amai said. "We should wait at least an hour for a response."

"Why?" Bryn asked. "If Ligon station received the call, they got it twenty minutes ago. They would have responded by now."

"Usually, but—"

"We're running out of time—Tina is running out of time," Bryn added, pointing to the door. "We need help and we're not getting it from Ligon station."

"It's risky," Amai said, looking down at the monitor.

"I think we risk more by staying silent for any longer," Bryn replied.

Amai had ignored Bryn's counsel before. She still didn't know what had happened—if they had been attacked, and by what—but maybe if Bryn had been in the cockpit with her, the ship would still be in one piece and two of her crew might still be alive. She would not make the same mistake again by ignoring Bryn's counsel and condemn them all to die, alone and suffocating in the vacuum of space. "You're right," she said. "I'll send it out at once."

\*\*\*

"How's your back?" Amai asked, almost exactly an hour after the last time she had posed the question to Bryn.

"A little better with every minute, but it's bad. I'm worried I may have broken something."

Amai stared at her with a blank expression before closing her eyes and whispering, "Fuck." She cradled her head in her hands, as she tried to fight off the thought that kept looping through her brain, as persistent and present as a song: *I shouldn't have left Tina.*

After Bryn woke up, Amai put her comm back in. She couldn't bring herself to speak, but she knew it was her duty to listen. She had left Tina back in section three, surrounded by nothing but cold metal and a dim, red glow. She was the only one left to listen.

But listening was excruciating.

The morphine Amai had given her had long worn off, so every time she woke up, she cried out in agony. Shrill, blood curdling screams that trailed off into soft weeping and small whispers of "Help" and "Please." And then there was silence as she passed out once again from the pain.

It took every ounce of Amai's control not to curl up in a ball and begin weeping every time Tina's voice surfaced over the comm. And then she looked over at Bryn, sitting on the ground quietly, oblivious to Tina's suffering. Bryn's comm had been damaged in the accident, such that it only transmitted—it no longer received. But every time Tina's comm clicked on with the sound of her voice, Amai saw Bryn's chin raise as static filled her ear. She knew Tina was speaking, but she had no idea what she was saying. And she never asked.

Amai had considered ripping the comm out of her own ear and shoving it into Bryn's, just so she would understand Tina's pain. So at least she would know that every second she sat on the floor waiting for her back to recover was another second that Tina had to continue with a lever in her back and the fear that no one would come to help her before she succumbed to the unimaginable pain. But Amai realized that she would only be spreading the pain that she felt from her own failure to help Tina. She had thought that there was time—that if she only could come back with some help that she could save her. If she had realized what going back for her would cost, maybe she would have spent more time coming up with a solution—maybe she could have figured out how to get her out of there on her own.

"How can I help you?" Amai asked, turning back to Bryn. "What else can I do?"

Bryn did a quick accounting of her injuries and said, "Nothing."

Amai heard Bryn's answer, but she couldn't sit still any longer, so she went rummaging through cabinets. She and Bryn had already eaten the protein bars stored in the medical kit, and she wasn't particularly hungry, but preparing food seemed like a good, helpful task.

The emergency rations were stored in the same cabinet as the emergency spacesuit, but fortunately they were not nearly as old. Amai had made a point of checking the dates on them yearly and replacing them as necessary; she always ate the ones that were going out of date, as she couldn't stand food going to waste. They weren't a gourmet meal by any means, but they were better than most prepackaged meal kits. Amai had always bought the top-of-the-line option, since she figured if she was ever in an emergency, she didn't want to have to suffer through eating too.

She poured a little water into each package, activated the heating element, and let them sit for ten minutes as they cooked themselves. Amai felt Bryn's eyes on her the whole time, watching her every movement across the cockpit. Amai supposed there was nothing else to do but watch her, but Bryn was examining her. Her captain had a specific plan in mind, and Bryn wasn't sure she was willing to follow it. Bryn watched Amai bend over, reach up, squat down. Amai was favoring her right side—her ribs and hips were bruised and tender.

Amai returned to Bryn with two packets. "Lasagna or curry?" she asked, trying to force a lightness into her voice.

"Lasagna," Bryn answered, taking the packet tentatively. The outside was cool to the touch, but steam flooded out the top of the package, warming the skin on Bryn's face. She ate slowly, savoring the taste and the warmth.

Amai ate several bites and then put her packet to the side.

Bryn's eyes flickered between her food and Amai. "What's wrong? Is it bad?"

"No, it's just—" Amai stopped, trying to articulate why she had stopped eating. It wasn't that she didn't like it—it was good. And once she started eating, she realized she was indeed hungry. But the taste, it was— "familiar."

Bryn cocked her head and continued eating. Between bites she added, "You've had it before?"

Amai frowned. "No...and yes. My father used to make something just like it. I'd forgotten about it until now."

Bryn paused mid bite. Amai wasn't looking at her—she wasn't looking at anything. Bryn saw an opening and she took it, "Did you grow up on the Vivaldi?"

"I was born on the Vivaldi," Amai said, a small smile creeping across her lips. "Where were you born?" Amai said, refocusing on Bryn.

"I was born in East Asia, in a town along the Yellow River. My family lived there for five years and then we moved to Australia until I was eleven. After that we moved to someplace in Europe for a year, and then over to North America until I graduated. We were always jumping from one place to another for my father's business."

"What business was he in?"

Bryn shrugged. "All sorts of things. Rice, carpets, cows, data. He was this perpetual entrepreneur. He would start a business and it would be wildly successful, until it wasn't." Bryn moved the thick noodles around in her packet without skewering any of them. "Then he would start a new one."

"But he always managed to start a new one?" Amai asked, hopeful.

"Yeah, he always did. Until he died at 49 of a heart attack."

"I'm sorry," Amai said, lowering her chin.

Bryn pursed her lips. "While I was growing up, all he ever talked about was how important work ethic was. If you just keep going, pushing, *fighting*—everything will work out. And when he died, I realized that the only value he tried to instill in me was the reason he died. You can't—" Bryn took a deep breath. "A person can't push in the throttle nonstop and expect to come out the other side of it all right. You have to let up at some point. There are times when you have to stop fighting or you won't survive. My father could never see that."

"And your mother?" Amai asked.

Bryn's somber expression gave way to a boisterous laugh. "Oh, she's the complete opposite. Cool as a cucumber, but I'll be goddamned if she ever accomplished a single thing in her life."

Amai laughed. "Well, she had you."

"Only because my dad pushed hard enough."

Bryn and Amai locked eyes and burst out laughing. Amai's ribs screamed back at her in protest, but Bryn didn't feel a thing through the anesthetic.

As Bryn's smile began to fade from her face she said, "I figured I'd try to split the difference between them with my own life. Accomplish some things, but not too many."

"How's that going?"

Bryn shrugged. "As long as we don't die here, I'd say I'm on track." Bryn took another bite of her lasagna. "What about your parents?"

"Oh, they were something," Amai said, wistfully. She didn't look at Bryn while she spoke. Amai stared out in front of her, as if she was looking straight into the past. "My mother was from South Africa, and my father was from the North. They both enlisted in the military right out of school and met in basic. They were assigned to different platoons, of course, but they sent each other letters the whole time. It was all very old fashioned.

"When they got married their contracts were up and they had the option to leave the military. But, if they stayed, they would be promoted and stationed on the Vivaldi together." Amai straddled between a frown and a smile. "It's hard to imagine now, but at the time the Vivaldi was something of a dream. A fully functioning colony, soaring through space and assisting in humanitarian missions—stranded ships, colony development, diplomatic missions. For two soldiers who had both seen the battlefield, it hardly seemed like a military assignment at all. They didn't hesitate to accept." Amai broke from her trance and looked back at Bryn. "Two years later they had me. And eight years after that the experiment that was the Vivaldi failed, nine AUs away from anyone who had the capacity to help."

For the first time since her ship had been hit, Amai felt tired. She'd been pushing forward, fueled by adrenaline and sheer force of will, but she had slowed down just long enough to feel the weight of the hours since she'd last slept. Combined with the aching bruises on her body, the need to sleep overwhelmed her.

"Let's get some sleep," she said, and Bryn was more than happy to oblige. Bryn simply laid down and wrapped the blanket that Amai had carried her in on around her shoulders.

Amai, on the other hand, had to rummage through cabinets to find something to rest her head on. The third cabinet she checked had an emergency space blanket. Amai unwrapped the thin, silver sheet as quietly as she could, but it crackled like wrapping paper from the moment she began to open it to the moment she laid down.

Amai's sleep wasn't filled with dreams, but with memories.

She dreamt of fire and screams. She saw people fall like flies as sirens blared around them. She savored her mother's kiss on her forehead and the final brush of her fingertips against her skin. She shivered against the cold metal of the cabinet walls, which grew colder with every passing hour. She let the darkness and silence overtake her as warm tears rolled down her cheeks.

Amai felt it all as if no time had passed at all. Once again, she was a helpless girl, trapped in a metal box, waiting for a savior that might never come.

## Chapter 7 - 5.08.2231
## 10:17, Earthtime

Bryn woke up to the sound of a soft beeping. Although it echoed throughout the room, it was so familiar that she hardly even noticed it.

Bryn sat up and rubbed her eyes. She stretched out her back and felt her muscles resist the tension, although she felt no pain. The anesthetic Amai applied had taken care of that at least.

It was only once Bryn recognized that she was not in her bed in the sleeping quarters, but on the floor of the cockpit, that the soft beeping of the console registered in her brain.

Bryn shot up, shedding off the thick blanket in one swift motion, and rushed over to the monitor. Her quick steps roused Amai, but before she could say anything Bryn had navigated through the screen— her fingers working more quickly than her memory— and a male voice filled the room.

"This is Ligon station hailing Captain Amai Menari of The Persika. Please respond. Expected delays must be reported to the Ligon station transit authority. Failure to report delays in a timely manner may result in a fine of 2,000 units. You have two hours to respond before incurring a penalty. This is Ligon station hailing Captain Amai Menari of The Persika..." The message continued on in a loop, over and over again. The man's nondescript voice filled the cabin so completely that Bryn was surprised to hear Amai laughing quietly behind her.

Bryn turned around to see her captain hunched over with the crinkled silver blanket still wrapped around her shoulders, and a smile on her lips.

It wasn't funny. Nothing about their situation was funny. But Amai couldn't quite process the utter hopelessness that had rushed over her, so she left her own mind and let her body take over. It rejected the intense rush of emotion and transformed it into a series of giggles and stomach spasms. And when Bryn looked at her with horror, Amai's body responded by laughing so hard it brought tears to her eyes.

"Why are you laughing?" Bryn asked, wondering where her captain had summoned her levity. Bryn's own limbs were heavy, as if they'd been filled with lead.

"I'm not sure," Amai said in between breaths. "I—I think I expected that message to say that they were coming for us. That they were on the way, and we would all be okay." Amai wiped a tear from the corner of her eye, as her laughing began to subside and the tension in her belly released. "But it's not going to be okay."

Bryn stared at her captain, her jaw clenched.

Amai met Bryn's eyes. "We're going to die out here."

"No," Bryn said, instinctively, still not releasing the tension in her jaw. "No, no we're not."

"Yes, we are," Amai said, her giggles gone, but her tone still light.

"They could still find us," Bryn said, her eyes darting to the oxygen readings: 28 hours remaining. They still had hours for someone to find them. They had hours to fix the comms. Hours to do something—anything to stay alive.

But Amai shook her head. "They're not even looking for us."

"Of course they are."

Amai finally stood up, shedding her silver blanket. The movement was labored, as she protected her left side. Her broken ribs were throbbing under her skin, but she was determined to endure the pain; all of their anesthetic was for Bryn. Amai leaned against the captain's chair. "We were originally supposed to return to Ligon Station at 09:15 on 5.08. At 10:15 they sent out a message, asking me to report our delay."

"So?" Bryn asked.

"So," Amai repeated, "they never received my message about our early departure from Io. They were still expecting us to arrive this morning, which means we still have about twenty-three hours before they even acknowledge that we're missing. And when they send someone out looking for us, they'll be looking along the route they have on file, expecting us to be stalled somewhere. It'll be weeks until they stumble upon us this far off course, if they find us at all."

Amai walked over to the window and looked out at the dark abyss. She touched the tips of her fingers to the glass and felt the cold that awaited her only a few inches away. But it was not the cold that sent shivers down her spine: it was Tina's cries.

She was awake again, and she was sobbing. Amai knew that she would go silent again in a few minutes; the pain would become too unbearable, and she would slip into unconsciousness. Amai had kept her comm in her ear, so she had heard each time Tina had repeated this cycle. Since she'd left her, Tina had awoken four times, and each time her cries were more desperate— her voice was a little weaker.

"Amai?" Tina asked softly.

Amai stared into the darkness as she reached up to her ear and activated her comm. "I'm here," she said.

Amai waited for a reply, but there was only silence on the other end of the comm. Amai wrapped her arms around her chest, her fingertips digging into her skin. She stared out the window for a long time as Bryn flitted from cabinet to cabinet, looking for a solution that didn't exist. When Amai turned around again, she had made up her mind.

*** 

"I'm going to get Tina." Amai looked over to Bryn as she pulled her suit over her thighs. "Are you coming?"

"What?" Bryn asked, incredulous.

"I can't leave her there any longer. I'm going to get her. It will be a lot easier if you come and help."

"Amai, you can't open the doors," Bryn said, instinctively moving toward the cockpit door to place herself between Amai and the exit.

"I'm going to have to in order to get Tina." Amai continued to put her suit on, pulling the sleeves up her arms one at a time.

"We'll lose two thirds of our oxygen if you open those doors."

"I know," Amai said. "But I can't leave Tina to die out there alone and in pain. We've left her out there for too long already."

"Amai, if you open those doors, she's going to die anyway. I'll die—you'll die! We'll all suffocate long before anyone can get to us." The pace of Bryn's words accelerated as Amai zipped up the front of her suit. "You need to give me time. Just a little bit of time—a few hours to try and figure this out. If you open those doors, we won't have enough time for someone to get to us. You'll be killing all of us."

Amai picked her helmet up and held it in her hands. "We're already dead, Bryn. The odds of someone happening upon us are one in a trillion, and we're going to run out of oxygen long before Ligon station finally sends a ship out looking for us."

"Just give me a little time—we can figure it out. *I* can figure it out."

Amai looked down at her helmet. The moment she heard the message, she knew that she would go to Tina, with or without Bryn's help. If she couldn't pull her off the lever, then she could at least give her a few shots of morphine and stay by her side, so she knew she wasn't going to die alone. She owed Tina that much. But Bryn was standing in front of her, begging for just a little bit of time. Did she owe that to Bryn too?

"Okay," Amai said, "you can have two hours."

"Thank you," Bryn said, lurching forward and grabbing Amai's gloved hands so tightly that she could feel the squeeze through the thick fabric. "I'm going to figure it out—I promise." Bryn didn't waste a moment in turning away from Amai and heading right to the monitor. Amai checked her watch, noting the time down to the second: 10:45:50. She hoped Tina would sleep through the whole two hours. And the next time Tina awoke, she wouldn't feel any pain at all.

***

Bryn worked frantically, trying to get the computer to boot up. The ship was running on reserve power, and as a result they'd been locked out of all secondary processes as life support systems were prioritized. The protocol had become standard after a ship of cargo runners had run out of power only a half hour before a relief ship could reach them by turning on the water heaters and booting up the entertainment systems. Twenty people died on account of boredom and a quick soak. After that, the programmers decided humans shouldn't have control of resources in emergency situations; the computer was better able to determine where power should be allocated in order to extend life support services maximally. And had the communications on the Persika been working properly, this system would have been optimal. They could have all just waited for their inevitable rescue. But the systems were not working, so Bryn had to figure out a way to override the fundamental protocol of the ship to fix whatever was broken in the code or identify the piece of hardware that was damaged. And she had to do it in under two hours.

If Bryn was a coder, she may have been able to do it; she would have known exactly what line of code would have given her access to manipulate the protocol to analyze its own code and search for anomalies. Or if she was a mechanic, maybe she would know what wire she could cut or panel she could manipulate to give her full access. But she was neither of these; she was just a pilot, desperate to stay alive.

After an hour and a half, Bryn had managed to divert some of the power from the lights to the console, so she could at least access the code concerning outgoing messages. The cockpit was only partially lit, a single light near the door throwing shadows throughout the rest of the room. Bryn poured over the code, only partly knowing what she was looking for. But there was so much of it—so many lines filled with jargon and commands she didn't quite understand. And she was only a quarter of the way through when Amai appeared behind Bryn. Her captain's shadow covered the entire monitor and Bryn looked at her over her shoulder, turning her head away from the monitor for the first time in two hours.

"Did you find anything?" Amai asked softly.

"No," Bryn said, and then corrected herself. "Not yet."

"I'm impressed you managed to open it at all."

"Just give me a few more hours," Bryn said, hearing the consoling tone in Amai's voice. "I'm only partway through, but I'm sure the error is in here. I just need to find it."

Bryn was lying, and Amai could hear it. Bryn didn't know that there was an error in the code. She didn't even know what the proper code was in order to identify an error. And Amai knew that if she gave her two more hours to comb through the code, they would be no closer to sending a message and the only person who would pay for it would be Tina, who would awake once more, screaming and alone.

"I'm going to get Tina. Are you coming?" Amai asked. All along she had hoped Bryn would come with her, because together they could get Tina off the machine. Alone, she might only hope to pump her with morphine and sit across from her as they waited for their time to run out.

Bryn closed her eyes and shook her head. "Amai, don't do this. Tina would want us to keep trying—to keep looking for a solution. If she was awake, she'd tell you that."

"Tina has been calling out my name and begging for help for *hours*," Amai said, her voice trembling. "I can't ignore her any longer, Bryn. I can't—not when no one is coming, and we have no way to hail them. I have a duty to Tina—"

"You have a duty to me too," Bryn interjected.

"Yes, I do," Amai acknowledged, "sometimes a captain's duties conflict. I can only do what I think is right. I'm sorry, Bryn." She paused for a moment before adding, "You should hold onto something."

Amai pulled her helmet over her head and locked it into place before turning away from Bryn and toward the door. She reached out her hand, ready to put her code in the keypad one more time, when she felt a strong tug on her left arm that pulled her backward and onto the floor.

The movement was so sudden that Amai didn't have an opportunity to brace herself. Her hip crashed into the hard, metal floor, sending a sharp pain all the way up her back, and her head bounced off the hard plastic of her helmet as it hit the ground. Amai had only managed to get her hands underneath her body to push herself up when she took a hard kick to the stomach. Amai's hands slipped beneath her, and her side returned to the ground. Her spacesuit had some padding, but not nearly enough to protect her from an outright assault on already broken ribs.

Amai looked up to see Bryn leaning over her. Her pilot reached down—this time not to strike, but to take off her captain's helmet. Bryn twisted it and the mechanism released. She pulled it off Amai's head and tossed it across the cockpit, all while staring at her captain. Bryn was breathing heavily, and sweat beaded on her temples, despite the increasing coldness in the cabin.

Amai stared back at her, trying to remain calm no matter how strongly her body cried out in panic. "What's the plan, Bryn? What now? Are you going to kill me?"

Bryn blinked quickly, breaking her eye contact with Amai. She shook her head and took a step back. "No—no."

Amai stood up slowly, hardly aware of the aching of her body. Her entire focus was on Bryn; she watched her facial expressions, the movements of her hands and feet, and the shifting of her eyes. Bryn was taller than Amai and had at least thirty pounds on her, but Amai had been trained in hand-to-hand combat when she served in the military. As long as she knew what she was up against, she could hold her own.

"I just can't let you go," Bryn said. Amai watched as a drop of sweat ran from Bryn's temple down to her chin, like rain on a windowpane. But Bryn didn't even know she was sweating.

"It's not your decision," Amai said, backing up a few centimeters at a time.

"Maybe it should be," Bryn said, closing the gap between them with a single step.

Bryn lowered her chin and clenched her right hand. She stepped forward with her left foot and hooked around her right fist, aiming to connect with Amai's head. It was the logical target—her head was the only part of her body that was exposed. Any blow Bryn landed on Amai's body would only be half as effective with the padding the spacesuit provided. So, of course she went for the head.

It was exactly as Amai expected.

In an instant, Amai moved her right foot back and bent her knees. She raised her left arm up to block Bryn's blow and grabbed her pilot's arm with her right hand. Amai shifted her weight onto her left foot and used every muscle in her lower body to break Bryn's stance and send her flying to the ground.

Bryn scrambled backward on her palms and shot back up. For the first time in hours, she felt her back spasm and a pain shoot up her spine. Bryn knew that if she could feel pain through the anesthetic, she must really be injured now. But her pain didn't matter; if she let Amai walk through the door to section two, then she would be dead long before her back began to heal.

Bryn expected Amai to advance, as most adversaries would do when they landed a blow. It was important to keep momentum going in a fight—to maintain the advantage. But her captain stood perfectly still. Her feet were rooted to the floor and her eyes were locked on Bryn, waiting. If Bryn had been more tactical, she may have waited as well. But Bryn was impulsive, and her adrenaline was through the roof. She moved toward Amai, every metallic footstep echoing through the cockpit.

This time, Bryn did not leave herself so open. She mirrored Amai's stance and tried to poke through her defenses with feints and quick jabs, but Amai deflected every blow. Back and forth they danced for several minutes, as their muscles fatigued and the pain in Bryn's back grew stronger.

Bryn searched for a window—for a singular weakness. And just as she thought she'd found it by feinting with her right arm and going for Amai's broken rib with her left, Bryn lingered a moment too long, and Amai found the opportunity she'd been waiting for. She grabbed Bryn's arm once again and then swept her right foot under Bryn's legs. Amai let go of her arm and let Bryn fall face-first onto the floor. Her jaw hit the metal with a sickening clang, and she struggled to push herself up onto her hands. Strands of Bryn's dusty brown hair clung to her face in a mixture of sweat and blood and she looked at Amai with large, pleading eyes.

"Please, Amai, don't do it," Bryn said.

Amai stood above Bryn. Her fists were still clenched. "I have to." She walked the length of the cockpit to get her helmet, and then she went straight to the door. Her body was exhausted, and it begged her to lie down and recoup. Every step was heavy with effort, but she was going to get Tina. It was something she should have done hours ago.

Amai had entered two of the four numbers of her code when she felt a searing pain in her back. The muscles in her body that had fought her to rest only moments before tensed up and cried out in terror. A warmth ran down her back and legs as the sharp sting gave way to throbbing.

Amai turned around to see Bryn with a knife in her hand.

It was red.

It was dripping.

Bryn's eyes were just as large as they had been when Amai turned away from her, but now they were not pleading with her—they were apologizing. Bryn said something, but Amai couldn't hear her through her helmet. The only thing she heard were her own labored breaths.

Amai felt her limbs growing weak; she felt a tremble in her knees.

But Tina was waiting. She was going to get Tina—finally.

Amai turned back around and entered her third number into the keypad. Her finger was hovering over the fourth as Bryn grabbed Amai's left shoulder and whipped her around. Amai stumbled backward, leaning against the door, and Bryn shoved the knife into the middle of her chest.

It wasn't a long knife—it was a utility knife; the kind they all kept in their pockets for minor tasks and emergencies. But it was long enough to slice through Amai's suit, skin, and aorta.

Amai stared at Bryn the whole time, as her fingers searched for the keypad beside her. Her right arm was stretched out until her entire body collapsed to the floor and it, too, fell limply by her side. She felt every muscle in her body relax as a warmth washed over her. And even though Bryn was standing in front of her, staring right at her, Amai died alone.

## Chapter 8 - 5.08.2231
## 12:54, Earthtime

As soon as the light left Amai's eyes, Bryn knew she needed to move her captain's body.

Amai was slumped up against the door, so it was only logical that she would need to move her at some point. It wouldn't do for her rescuers to open the door, only to have a body fall to their feet. It was also prudent to move her before the rigor mortis set in, and her limbs stiffened.

These were the reasons Bryn gave herself for deciding to move Amai's body; they were logical and reasonable, and they kept her from facing the truth: she could feel Amai's eyes on her.

Her captain's eyes were glazed over and vacant, but they were locked onto Bryn's eyes, and even when she turned her back, Bryn could feel them upon her. They were accusing her of the heinous crimes of mutiny and betrayal—and murder. All crimes Bryn was unwilling to answer for, so long as only 26 hours of oxygen remained on the ship. So Bryn pushed the thoughts from her mind by moving her captain's body, eyes and all.

In only a moment's time Bryn knew that there was only one reasonable place to put her. She could not shove her in a cabinet or pull her to the side and leave her on the ground, slumped over. Bryn had killed her captain, but she still respected her. And even in death, Amai deserved a position of respect in the cockpit.

Bryn carried Amai over to the captain's chair with ease. Adrenaline still surged through her body, and Amai seemed almost weightless; even through her spacesuit, she seemed so thin that Bryn thought she might break her bones if she held her too tightly. And still, Amai had beaten her in hand-to-hand combat.

Blood flowed from the slit in the back of Amai's suit and onto Bryn's jumpsuit. Bryn's skin broke out in goosebumps as the warm fluid seeped through the fabric and touched her belly. With every step, more blood flowed from Amai to Bryn, soaking through her suit all the way down to her shoes.

Bryn laid Amai in the chair gently, but as she stepped back Amai's head lolled forward and her entire body pulled away from the chair. Bryn jumped forward and kept her captain upright. She managed to keep her seated by removing her helmet and allowing her body to slump down in the chair. Although her eyes stayed wide open, still vacant and accusatory, they were now looking at the vastness of space, instead of right at Bryn.

As Bryn stepped back, she felt a small bit of relief. Amai's lifeless body and the trail of blood painting the floor of the cockpit would not let Bryn forget what she'd done, but she thought she might be able to ignore them enough now to continue combing through the code.

Amai was dead, but she wouldn't let her die in vain. Bryn promised herself that she would get out of this alive with the time Amai's death bought her. She sat down at the console and continued reading through the code, line after line, as meticulously as she could. She knew somewhere, there had to be something she could fix. There had to be an error somewhere that she could correct. Because if there wasn't, then no one would find her. And she wasn't ready to die.

\*\*\*

Bryn went through the code three times and found nothing at all. On the second attempt, she had begun picking at a mole on her left hand, and by the end there was nothing but a crater in her skin and an overwhelming sense of dread.

"It has to be something...there has to be something," Bryn whispered to herself over and over. She alternated between pacing the length of the cockpit and sitting back at the monitor, looking at random sections of code. Bryn tried to remain calm, but she was sweating through her suit. Bryn had stripped the top half off, letting it hang around her waist, but a thin layer of sweat still clung to her skin. It mixed with Amai's blood on her stomach, turning her white tank top a shade of pink. In a room that most would have worn three layers of clothing to protect against the chill, Bryn could have mistaken it for a sauna.

Bryn had been pacing near the door—out of sight of Amai, who always hated Bryn's displays of anxiety—when she heard a static fill her ear. Bryn stopped in her tracks. The static came on strong and then disappeared, only to return a moment later. Bryn reached up to her ear, her fingers shaking and clumsy, and struggled to remove her earpiece. It was a little thing that fit right in the concha, but she hadn't bothered to remove it because it felt so natural now. It was as much a part of her as her hair or fingernails. Her comm had been damaged in the accident, so she had been hearing nothing but a faint static on and off for the last day and a half. But every time she'd heard static, Amai had heard Tina.

Bryn pulled the comm from Amai's ear carefully. She tried not to look into her captain's eyes as she removed it, but she couldn't help it—they were staring right at her. Now they accused her of a different crime. Bryn could hear the criticism, as clear as if Amai had said it herself, *You condemned Tina to die a horrible death when you killed me, but you're going to use her to save yourself, aren't you?*

"Maybe," Bryn answered, her voice echoing in the hollow silence. She curled her fingers around Amai's comm and stepped away from her—away from her gaze.

Bryn fumbled with the little earpiece before securing it in her right ear, exactly where the other one had been. It slid into the small indentation her original comm had carved out after years of uninterrupted use. With a single touch, Bryn turned the comm on synced frequencies with the receiver in her head, and she was met with silence. Bryn counted the beats, waiting to hear Tina's voice, but there was nothing.

Bryn activated the comm. "Tina?" she said, uncertainty in her tone. "Tina, are you there?"

There was more silence and Bryn felt little beads of sweat surface on her temples.

"Amai?"

A smile broke through on Bryn's face for the first time in hours. "Tina!" she said.

"Amai…" Tina answered. Her voice was weak.

"Tina, it's Bryn," she said quickly. "Listen, I need your help."

"Where's Amai?" Tina asked, barely enunciating her words.

Bryn hesitated. "She's injured."

"How?"

"In the accident. Listen, Tina, I need your help. Is there somewhere in the cockpit, anywhere where there's some hardware that controls the communication system. Like a circuit board or a panel or something like that?" Bryn spoke quickly, her heart racing. She only breathed when she stopped talking, but her heavy breaths were uninterrupted.

"Tina?" Bryn asked. She waited, but there was no response. "Tina!" Bryn screamed, but there was only silence on the other side of the comm.

Bryn brought her hands to her head and pulled at her hair. "Fuck!" she yelled. She had the urge to rip the comm out of her ear and throw it to the ground, but she restrained herself. Amai had mentioned Tina passing out—something about waking up and losing consciousness again. Maybe she had just passed out again. Bryn prayed she wasn't dead. She really needed her to not be dead.

Bryn couldn't sit down. She moved around the cockpit, opening cabinets and pulling things out before unceremoniously stuffing them back in. She managed to find a toolkit buried behind the rations and within an hour she'd laid out all of her available tools on the floor, organized according to size. She even tore apart the med kit Amai had been treating her with and integrated those supplies with the tools. While she was at it, she gave herself a shot of anesthetic. Between the accident and her fight with Amai, Bryn suspected she may have broken something in her back, or maybe slipped a disc, but now wasn't the time to feel that pain. She didn't want to feel anything at all, so she gave herself a dose and a half, just to get ahead of the agony she knew awaited her. Then Bryn organized all the food she had left by preference. She had far more food than she needed— enough to last almost a month—which is why she felt the need to organize it. If she was going to be eating some of her last meals, she didn't want to be eating StarFarms' meatloaf cabbage rolls when Orion's coconut lime chicken was available.

Each of these tasks Bryn did quietly and slowly, moving as if she was underwater, to ensure she would hear even the slightest whimper from Tina if one was uttered. Even though her movements were controlled and required little exertion, the thin layer of sweat across Bryn's forehead never dried out, and her heart never stopped racing.

Bryn was kneeling over a nearly empty roll of bandages when she heard Tina wake up. Her body straightened out as she shot up and Bryn put her hand to her ear instinctively. "Tina," Bryn said softly, trying and failing to hide her anxiety. "Tina, it's Bryn," she said.

"Bryn," Tina said, breathing heavily. "Where's Amai?"

"We don't have time, Tina," Bryn said. The last time Tina was awake—from the time Bryn first heard the static in her ear to when Tina went quiet in her ear—she was conscious for less than two minutes. Bryn could hear her seconds ticking away with every labored breath.

"Listen, I'm trying to save us. I need to know if there's any hardware that controls the communications system in the cockpit. Is there a panel or a circuit board or anything—anything that could be damaged?"

Tina took a few breaths, wincing with each one, as she thought. "Yeah," she finally said. "On the starboard side—" Tina's voice trailed off.

"Tina!" Bryn yelled into the comm. This time, her voice brought Tina back.

Tina cried out, as she jolted back to consciousness. Then she laughed. "Fuck, Bryn. I'm dying."

"Tina, we have to get a message out or we'll both die. Where's the panel?" Bryn yelled, the softness in her voice gone.

"The middle panel...on the starboard side. There's a cluster of yellow and blue wires—check those."

Bryn walked over to the starboard side of the cockpit. There were three panels built into the wall, almost invisible in the partial light, but as Bryn ran her fingers over the metal, she noticed the miniscule gaps where the panel met the rest of the ship—and she felt the screws.

"What am I looking for?" Bryn asked, heading back to the tools she's laid out across the floor, looking for a screwdriver.

"I don't know," Tina said. Her tone was low and muffled, and Bryn realized she was speaking through gritted teeth, trying to stay awake. "Any frayed or snapped wires."

Bryn spotted a screwdriver and rushed back to the panel. She was relieved to find she didn't need to adjust the head and worked quickly to remove each screw with the hope that once she was looking at the wires, she would still have someone there to tell her what they meant. She narrated her progress to Tina. "One screw out...two more...just hold on." And in return Tina grunted into her comm to let Bryn know she was still awake.

Bryn pulled off the panel to reveal more wires than she ever could have expected. "It's open," Bryn said, scanning the wires looking for the ones that were yellow and blue. The small flashlight that had been in the toolkit was nearly as bright as a sun, and she had to squint against the brightness until her eyes adjusted. It also didn't help that many of the bundles looked alike—yellow and green, blue and white. In the bottom right corner of the panel, Bryn finally found it: a cluster of yellow and blue wires. "I see them," Bryn said, running her fingers along the individual wires, looking for one that was frayed or cut. But they all seemed perfectly fine.

"They're all okay," Bryn said, feeling her heart sink in her chest.

There was silence for a moment, and Bryn thought Tina must have passed out again, but with great effort Tina responded, "Check the transmitter."

Bryn looked back down at the wires. When she followed them up, they went out of sight, to a part of the ship she couldn't hope to access, but at the bottom of the panel they fed into a black box with no discernable features. "How do I check it?" Bryn asked, running her fingers around it, searching for a button or something.

"Make sure all three lights are on."

"Lights?" Bryn said, seeing nothing.

"At the back," Tina said, stopping to wince. "The control panel. You can reset it there."

Bryn parted the wires to see the panel Tina was talking about. There were three lights, indicating the operational status of the three main components of communication: satellite, hardware, and transmitting. The first two were lit up a bright green, and the last one was off. "I see it. The transmitter isn't on."

"Reset it. Hold the button for ten seconds."

Bryn did exactly as Tina instructed. She opened the guard and pressed the little red reset button and watched as the light turned off and then one at a time they lit back up: green, green, and green. Bryn leapt up and cried out with joy.

"Tina, you did it. You goddamn genius, you did it!"

Tina breathed out a laugh, but she was in too much pain to join Bryn in her joy.

Bryn knelt back down to close the reset guard, but as soon as she moved the wires aside, she realized that now only two of the green lights were glowing: satellite and hardware. In an instant, the relief Bryn had felt was replaced by panic. "Tina," she said, her voice shaking. "It's off."

"What?"

"It was green, but now it's off again." Without even waiting for Tina's instruction, Bryn initiated the process again. She held the button and watched their communications go offline, only to come back one by one, green and operational. Except twenty seconds after the transmitter came back online, it dropped again. Bryn explained the situation to Tina, biting at the skin on her lips.

"There's probably a short somewhere. I'm sorry."

Bryn waited for more, for her next step, but Tina was asleep. Bryn sat next to the open panel with her head in her hands and wept. Her tears mingled with her sweat, and for the first time since she killed Amai she realized how cold it was in the cockpit. Bryn pulled up her jumpsuit and shivered as her whole body convulsed with the strength of her sobs. She cried until she was exhausted, both physically and mentally. And, still sitting up, she closed her eyes and slept.

Bryn dreamt herself back onto Io, looking out at Jupiter. The sunburnt sands that swept across the planet promised to envelop her. The rest of her crew was alive and laughing; even Amai, who hardly ever laughed. She thought she might just stay there, on Io. How pleased she was when the others agreed. Bryn smiled and felt like a great weight had been lifted—they would all be safe if they just stayed on Io.

\*\*\*

Bryn ate a little and then vomited it up. She was able to keep water down, so she drank a full bottle and then started the task of following the wires as far as she possibly could. If there was a short, Bryn was going to find it.

Despite all of her hours—years—in the cockpit of the Persika, Bryn had never realized the walls were lined with panels. They were well hidden, seamlessly implanted into the walls. And Bryn had never taken much time to look at the walls; her attention was always drawn forward, out into space.

But now Bryn became intimately familiar with the panels embedded in the walls. They were all shapes and sizes, according to their position within the ship, but most were about a meter by a meter of 1mm thick metal, secured with four screws—one in each rounded corner. Bryn simply started by following the wires. She removed the panel immediately above the first, and upon finding the wires completely intact, she removed the one above that. She had to stand on her tiptoes to reach the top screws and then she stepped up onto the thin, horizontal frame between the first two panels to examine the wires; Bryn was grateful that it held her weight without issue. The metal was thin, but it was strong.

The wires took a turn to the left and then snaked downward until Bryn was pulling up panels from the floor. She was relieved when the wires passed behind Amai's chair, clear of the pool of blood that had slowly formed underneath her. Bryn was halfway to the other side of the ship, on her hands and knees, following the yellow and blue wires with her fingertips when she heard Tina come alive again over the comm.

Once again, she asked for Amai, and once again Bryn avoided the question.

"I've been looking for the short," Bryn said, still checking the wires she'd just unearthed.

"What short?" Tina asked.

"You said it was probably a short with the wiring."

"I did?" Tina's voice sounded far away.

"Yeah."

"Oh…" Tina paused, and some hint of recollection returned to her. "Did you check the transmitter?"

"Yes, it seemed fine, but the transmission light won't stay on."

"So, it might be a short," Tina repeated. She paused and Bryn set to unscrewing another panel. "What about the connections between the wires and the transmitter? Did you check those?"

Bryn sat up. "No." She crawled over to the original panel, her joints now accustomed to being on the floor, and started to check the connection of the wires. She had to lift the black box up and bring her head down to the ground to see the entry point of the wires. "They look okay," Bryn said after some careful examination. She put the box down as well and added, "What about this black box? Is there something I should check on it?"

"Black box?" Tina asked, the pain in her voice giving way to curiosity.

"Yeah, the black box all the wires go into just before they connect with the transmitter."

"There is no black box," Tina said, matter-of-factly.

Bryn furrowed her eyebrows. "I'm looking right at one."

"I don't know what that is," Tina whispered.

"What?" Bryn said, her eyes widening.

"I don't know what..." Tina trailed off, leaving Bryn staring at the black box.

Bryn had two courses of action: she could continue pulling up panels on the ship, searching the wires for some sort of damage, or she could try and open the black box that Tina thought shouldn't be there. It would be another hour or two before Tina woke up again, delirious from the pain and asking for Amai, before Bryn could confirm how certain she was that the box shouldn't be there. It was a little thing; it would be easy to forget, especially in a state of distress. What if it was important and Bryn broke it by accident? She might ruin any of her chances of ever sending a distress signal. But Tina had been right about everything else, from the color of the wires to the location of the transmitter. Why should she doubt her now?

Bryn reached forward and ran her fingers over the outside of the box, hoping to find a button or clasp that would pop it open and let her see inside, but there wasn't any clear way to open it. When she shined a light on it, she noticed a seam running right down the middle. It was almost invisible, but it was something. Bryn pulled out her knife, wedged it into the seam, and began to wiggle it back and forth. She tried not to look at the blade. After she used it last, she had hastily wiped it on her jumpsuit to remove Amai's blood, but she hadn't looked at it. Most of the metal was clean, but there were places near the hilt and along the top of the blade where patches of dried blood remained. The reminder only made Bryn work faster. She pushed her blade in deeper and moved it more quickly, trying to pry the halves of the black box apart.

She pushed her knife in deeper once more and the box cracked and split apart. Bryn threw her knife to the floor and it slid across the room, crashing into the other supplies she'd laid out neatly and scattering them into disarray. Bryn didn't notice though—she was focused only on the contents of the box. Most of the wires were untouched; they simply ran from one side of the box to the other. But there were three wires that had been cut and reattached to a small device, no larger than a marble. The entire device pulsed a bright blue every two seconds and Bryn's breath caught in her chest. She reached out and pulled it up to her face, examining it from every angle, just to be sure.

She had seen a device like this one before, in what felt like another lifetime. Her father had brought it home tucked away in his pocket; the neon blue light cut right through his trousers and drew her attention.

When he pulled it out, she was surprised at how small it was. Bryn held it in her fingers, right in front of her eyes and examined it carefully. "What is it?" she'd asked.

"It's the reason we're moving," he'd said, and he was true to his word. Bryn later learned from her mother that it was a disruptor. Someone in her father's business had planted it on one of his automated lines, shielded from view within a false copper pipe. It shut down production for nearly a month. Her father and his team brought in specialists and bought expensive replacement parts for things that weren't even broken. Her father's most successful business was sabotaged, and there was nothing for them to do but pick up and move once again, this time to Europe where he had his eyes on a vertical farm.

But Bryn's eyes were locked on the disruptor. She had found the source of the issue—a problem she could fix with a few quick snips of wire and a pair of pliers. Yet, her heart did not swell with joy. Bryn knew she was no closer to being saved than she was just a moment before. In fact, she may have been more likely to die.

She looked back to Amai, slumped in her chair and staring vacantly ahead. "I should have let you go to Tina," Bryn said. For the first time since she had killed Amai, Bryn felt true, unquestionable regret. For hours, she'd churned inside every time she thought of Amai's face. Bryn was disgusted with herself, but she knew she had killed her captain for a *reason*. It was self-preservation—it was Amai's life or hers. But now Bryn knew she may have killed her for nothing. She had robbed Amai of her last hours of life and subjected Tina to unspeakable pain, all to realize that there was someone out there blocking their communications—withholding salvation.

There was someone keeping them in darkness, hoping it would envelop them.

There was someone who wanted them dead.

\*\*\*

Bryn removed the disruptor with two snips and rejoined the wires by stripping back the rubber and twisting them together with pliers. Once she had decided to do it, the process only took her about two minutes. She watched as the transmitting light flickered on a brilliant green and then she stared at it for several minutes, just to make sure it didn't turn off again.

The disruptor hadn't left Bryn's hand since she discovered it, and it was no different once it was disconnected. The wires were embedded into the smooth surface—both fluid and solid at the same time—so Bryn cut them down as close to the surface as she could. She ran her fingers over them, until she couldn't feel the tingle of their bristles on her skin.

Eventually the disruptor swallowed them, leaving the surface slick and flawless. It still glowed neon blue, and when Bryn finally put it in her pocket it shined clear through her jumpsuit. In a different circumstance, she would have smiled.

Of course, there were disruptors that did not glow bright blue, but they were inferior to the one in Bryn's pocket. Produced on the black market, they always had some sort of drawback; the range was short, or they died unexpectedly. Some of them were even known to spontaneously explode. The only reliable disruptor was the one produced by Intelitec, and after only a single generation of the technology, regulators had insisted on a myriad of features to prevent it from being used maliciously, one of which was the bright blue glow it emitted. Unfortunately, a simple black box made of two-centimeter-thick titanium was enough to get around such inconveniences. That was, as long as no one who knew what they were looking at stumbled upon it.

Bryn wondered how long the disruptor had been there. It could have been weeks or months; at least since Tina had last laid eyes on the transmitter, and Bryn had no idea when that would have been. But Bryn was certain that it had only been activated after they landed on Io. She had watched Amai send a message to the Company, notifying them of the ship's on time arrival on Io, and she'd heard the Company reply back with, "Arrival confirmed." After that, she couldn't be sure if any of Amai's messages had made it through; she hadn't heard her send or receive any of them.

The fact that the disruptor had only been activated after they left Io was confirmation enough for Bryn that when the ship was hit, it wasn't an accident. They had been attacked and their communication had been shut off in anticipation of that attack. Why they had been attacked at all was something Bryn couldn't quite confirm.

The Company may have had an interest in keeping Gabe's death quiet and destroying the Persika would allow them to cover it up. But the risk to them was substantial. If anyone discovered they had attacked a ship under their commission, the Company would face fire from without and within. The government would get involved, the media would tear them to shreds, and every commissioned ship under their flag would find work somewhere else.

It was also possible that they were the target of a robbery. The platinum ore they were mining was worth more than most people made in a lifetime. It would have been easy enough to give the guard a hundred units to slip onto the ship while they were out in Ligon station for a chance to install the disruptor, and a tracker while they were at it. But Bryn had never heard of thieves tearing through a ship to grab their prize; they were more likely to threaten their targets with high-powered lasers—or actually shoot them, although that was rare.

Or maybe someone just wanted them dead, for a personal vendetta or an unpaid debt. Other than Amai and Tina, Bryn did not know much about her other crewmates. It's possible that they had gotten caught in the middle of a gang rivalry or a hit.

All of these potentials made Bryn's next steps much harder to calculate. Unfortunately, she was low on oxygen, and therefore low on time; any rescue out of Ligon station wouldn't reach them before they suffocated. Bryn had to send out a mayday call and hope someone responded. If she knew, with absolute certainty, who had attacked her, then she could craft her message to increase the likelihood of being rescued—and reduce the chances of their attackers coming back to finish the job. But all she knew was half the ship was missing and there was a disruptor in her pocket. It was not enough to go on.

Bryn racked her brain as she prepared her body. She knew the statistics on mayday calls: any given ship had a 39% greater likelihood of rescue when the distress call was issued over video compared with audio alone. The video capabilities of the Persika were still intact, so Bryn prepared herself for the camera. She scrubbed her fingers and cleaned her face. She did her hair and hid her injuries. Bryn did all the things the textbook said to do, and then she prayed.

She practiced her words at least ten times before she recorded. Bryn stared at her own reflection, trying to control her facial expressions and remain calm. It was a necessary step in order to come across as genuine, because her words were full of lies. Bryn knew it was her best chance at survival, regardless of who had attacked them.

After straightening her shoulders and softening her expression, Bryn reported that she was the only surviving member of the Persika. That she didn't know what had hit them. And that Amai had died from trying to repair the ship, instead of at Bryn's own hands. It was a vague message that painted Bryn as confused and uninformed, which is exactly what Bryn had hoped it would be. If someone thought she was in a position to point a finger upon her rescue, she wouldn't be rescued at all. Even worse, she might be killed. Bryn needed to seem like the innocent victim, caught in the crossfire. Or at least that's what she thought she needed to do.

Bryn sent out the message, and then she continued with the cleansing of her body. She had killed Amai ten hours ago, but her captain's blood still covered her. Bryn focused so fully on getting the comms working that she had hardly noticed it, but now that the work was done—the message was out and there was nothing else she could do—Bryn's attention turned to the blood on her skin—Amai's blood. She scrubbed her hands and changed her clothes, but no amount of scrubbing made her feel truly clean.

Eventually, when Bryn's hands were raw and red, she accepted that she may never feel clean again. Maybe that was something she deserved.

Bryn sat down for the first time in hours. She lowered herself carefully into the chair in front of the console, next to the captain's chair that Amai was slumped over in. Someone else may have mistaken her captain for sleeping, but Bryn could not forget that she was dead. She could not forget that she was sitting in the wrong chair and the world had been changed forever.

Bryn brought her feet up into the chair and held onto her knees. She stared out ahead, into the darkness of space littered with bright stars; each one held its own promise of life and opportunity, but Bryn was so far from all of them. She was in the darkness, waiting for someone—anyone—to come pull her out.

## Chapter 9 - 5.09.2231
## 02:56, Earthtime

Bryn was exhausted, but she couldn't sleep. She only had twelve hours of oxygen left. How could she sleep her final hours away?

Two hours after Bryn sent the mayday call, she started to get nervous. After three hours with no response, Bryn began to pace the length of the cockpit, mindlessly stepping around pulled up panels and scattered emergency supplies. At four hours, she was slumped back in her chair, staring out into space and picking at her cuticles.

She hummed a song to fill the silence. It was an old jazz song that her mother used to sing while folding laundry or organizing the garage, whenever she was doing mindless things. She'd always tried to get Bryn to sing along with her, but Bryn was content to listen to her mother sing. She never wanted to open her mouth and ruin the rhythm.

But there was nothing to ruin on the cockpit of the Persika, except the sting of silence.

"Bryn?" a voice said, so loud and clear it drowned out Bryn's own humming.

"Tina," Bryn replied, refocusing her eyes and bringing herself back to reality. "You're alive!" A smile spread across Bryn's lips. She had begun to fear the worst for her mechanic.

"I guess so."

The smile slowly faded from Bryn's face. "You were right about the box. It was a disruptor. Someone was blocking our communications." Bryn waited for a reply, but when Tina said nothing she added, "I sent out a distress call four hours ago."

"Is anyone coming?" Tina asked, her voice completely flat.

"No," Bryn said. Then she added, "At least, not yet."

Tina coughed and cried out as her body contorted and pain cascaded through her torso.

Bryn winced. Every time she heard Tina cry out, she felt a stone drop in her stomach. They piled on top of one another, sinking deeper and deeper inside of her. But she could not get rid of them now; instead, they weighed her down so completely that she was rooted in place, stuck in the cockpit until someone came to rescue her or she suffocated. She could not justify opening the doors now, not after all she'd done to keep them closed.

Tina sighed. Bryn listened to each breath, more labored than the last. "You know," Tina finally said. "I used to think I would live forever."

Bryn laughed and a smile spread across her lips. "Sure, me too, at least when I was a teenager."

"No, really," Tina said, her voice muted by a thin layer of static over the comm. "The first time I heard about the cybernetic transplants, I thought, *there's no way to die anymore.* I figured if I was ever injured on the job, or if I got cancer from mining uranium on a shit job, they could just fix me up. Why would anyone ever die anymore?"

Bryn stared straight ahead, trying not to look at Amai. Trying not to think of Gabe.

"Still, people kept dying all the time—it hardly slowed down at all. With all the tech, less than half a percent of mortalities were ever averted. And even then, I thought, *But not me. I won't die...*Why did I think that, Bryn? Why did I think that it would never be me?"

Bryn gripped the armrest on her chair until her knuckles turned white. She clenched her teeth so hard a vein began throbbing in her neck.

Tina breathed in sharply, and a sob rose in her throat. "Every time I wake up, the blood beneath my feet has spread out a little farther. I'm watching myself die, and there's nothing I can do to stop it."

In the silence, the static grew, almost as loud in Bryn's head as Tina's voice. But when Tina spoke again, Bryn didn't notice the static. All she heard was Tina, as loud and clear as if she was standing right in front of her: "What happened to Amai?"

Bryn closed her eyes and breathed in deeply. She sat there, the breath stuck in her lungs, for what felt like an eternity. But when she finally let it out, she also released the tension in her jaw enough to respond, "I killed her." Bryn turned her head to the right, and when she opened her eyes again, she was staring at Amai. Her captain was frozen in time, just as Bryn had left her, slumped down in her chair, staring ahead into space, all of her blood that wasn't on Bryn's jumpsuit pooled beneath her. Now that Bryn was looking at her, she couldn't take her eyes away. "We'd already be dead, all three of us—hours ago—if I hadn't done it."

"You fucking monster," Tina said, the vitriol in her voice almost imperceptible against the grain of the static. "How could you?"

Bryn looked at her hands, where little threads of red had seeped so deep into her skin that she couldn't scrub them off. "I had no choice," she said, finally saying the words aloud that she'd been repeating within her head since she'd first slipped the blade into Amai's back. "I had no choice."

Static flooded the comm, overwhelming any words that Tina was saying, if she was talking at all. Bryn only heard the white noise, and still, somehow, it was worse than the silence.

## Chapter 10 - 5.09.2231
## 12:53, Earthtime

Bryn's eyes were bloodshot. She refused to sleep, and in her efforts to stay awake she kept her eyes open wide. Bryn hardly blinked for fear that if she closed her eyes for even a second too long, she might never open them again.

The ship had two hours of oxygen remaining, and if she slept, she would suffocate slowly and silently. But Bryn had no intention of going peacefully. She had decided long ago that she would go out fighting, even if that meant gasping for air that wasn't there.

Bryn had spent the last two hours alternating between staring out into space and checking the monitor for a response to her distress call. The latter was only a neurotic action—if there was a reply, the console would alert her. Nonetheless, Bryn compulsively checked it, sure that someone would reply; she was sure someone would come save them, just in time. *Someone had to.*

The intermediate static in her comm let Bryn know that Tina was still alive.

The acrid scent slowly filling the cockpit told her that Amai had started to decompose.

The chill in her bones indicated the heating components were beginning to fail.

The taste of blood in her mouth reminded her that she might not be able to move her legs once the anesthetic wore off.

Bryn used all of her focus to block out each of these sensations and stared straight ahead at the distant stars. All of Bryn's other senses reminded her that she was trapped on a doomed ship, but her eyes could be deceived. Out in space there was nothing but possibility—planets, moons, and asteroids all dying to be rediscovered by her. If Bryn only focused on what she saw, she could almost forget the reality that surrounded her.

She imagined herself on Neptune, wearing an insulated suit and taking samples for one of the biotech companies—a far more noble undertaking than working for the Company. Bryn had always admired scientists, but she had never considered herself academic enough to pursue that route. Now that seemed like such a mistake.

Bryn was picturing herself taping a label onto the vial of a new specimen on Neptune when reality cut into her line of sight: fast approaching from the starboard side was a ship.

Bryn leaned forward and blinked several times, clearing the blur from her dry eyes. Her heart leapt when the object did not disappear, and a wide smile stretched across her face. She watched as it approached, advancing from a speck in the vast emptiness to a huge freighter, slowing as it approached.

The smile on Bryn's lips slowly disappeared as goosebumps cascaded over her skin, originating from the top of her spine and spreading out until they reached her fingertips. With near certainty, Bryn recognized it as the freighter she had seen coming at them after Io—the one she had narrowly avoided before being removed from the cockpit by Amai.

Bryn tore her eyes from the ship and turned to the console. She checked for any communication, but there was nothing. The approaching ship had not responded to the mayday call, as was standard procedure. Instead, it had merely shown up.

Bryn turned on the local communication channel. She hesitated for a moment before speaking, "This is Bryn Michaels of the Persika. Approaching ship, identify yourself."

She waited, watching the ship slowly come forward. It was a behemoth, at least three times the size of the Persika, when it had been intact. But no one answered her.

Bryn repeated herself, "This is Bryn Michaels of the Persika. Approaching ship, identify yourself." And still, there was no reply.

As the ship drew closer, Bryn noticed that it had been scrubbed clean of any insignias or identifying marks. It was painted an unimposing slate gray, and the body was unremarkable and commonplace. Asked to give a description of the ship, an average person would not have been able to state anything of note to distinguish it from most other ships, but Bryn recognized it. Before Amai hired her, Bryn had worked on a ship just like it—a ship that belonged to the Company.

Bryn closed her eyes and hung her head. They hadn't responded to the distress call, and they weren't answering her inquiries because they didn't want any record of their presence.

Bryn had sent the wrong message in her mayday call.

When Bryn looked up again, the rear of the ship was suspended over the window of the cockpit and there was a loud bang as the gate from the other ship attached to the emergency hatch in section two.

Bryn activated her comm. "Tina, I don't know if you can hear me, or if you're even alive, but we're being boarded. I don't think they're here to rescue us. I'm sorry for everything. I'm really sorry." Bryn pulled her hand from her ear as a loud bang resonated throughout the ship. The emergency hatch in section two had been opened, and the metal floor clanged again and again as several pairs of heavy feet dropped down into the ship.

There were at least four of them. Only an hour ago Bryn would have been overjoyed at the sound of footsteps just outside her door, but now they caused her to panic; her muscles contracted and her breaths quickened, as some deep-seated instinct prepared her to fight for her life. Her eyes searched the cockpit for a weapon, darting from a fire extinguisher to the oxygen tank, but she finally spotted her knife hidden amongst the supplies she laid out on the floor. It was a small blade, but she knew it was deadly at close range. And it was really all she had.

Bryn waited to the left of the door, her knife drawn and her feet staggered. But as the seconds ticked by, nothing happened.

Bryn lowered her hands and took a step back. She was about to turn around, back toward the console, when there was a light tapping on the cockpit door.

Two knocks—as if it was late at night and they were checking to see if she was still awake. Bryn's muscles tensed up anew, but she didn't say anything.

Nearly thirty seconds passed before they knocked again, with a more assertive hand. "Bryn Michaels, we're here to answer your distress call," a voice said. It was clear and crisp, projected through an external microphone.

Bryn swallowed, but she didn't answer. She knew they were talking amongst themselves, within the safety and silence of their spacesuits, deciding exactly what they should say in order to get her to open the door. They could enter via the emergency hatch, but the doors on the ship were sealed and would only open with the code she and Tina knew. Otherwise, they would have to force their way in.

"Bryn Michaels, we received your distress call. We're here to rescue you."

She wanted to believe him. She wanted so badly to believe him. A tear escaped her eyes and streamed down her face. "Who are you?" she asked, betraying every one of her instincts.

There was a pause. It only lasted ten seconds, but ten seconds was far too long a pause for such a simple question. "We're from the starship Bernia, moving some cargo out toward Reiner station. We just heard your distress call as we were passing by."

"Who do you work for?"

Another pause. "We're on a government contract."

Bryn moved her jaw up and down as she tried to steady her hands. "That's a Company ship," she finally said.

"Maybe it used to be, but not anymore." His tone was calm and even. Bryn felt like he was trying to talk her off a ledge.

"Why didn't you respond to the call? Why didn't you identify yourself when you approached?" Bryn asked, the edge in her voice sharpened by the emotion she was trying to keep at bay.

There was no hesitation this time. "What? We did. Maybe there's something wrong with your receiver."

Bryn felt her defense crack. She had spent so many hours trying to fix the transmitter that she hadn't given a second thought to the receiver. It had been working hours ago, when Amai was still alive and Ligon station had messaged them, but the ship hadn't received a message since then. What if something had happened to the receiver? She had no way to check. Or at least no way to check without the help of Tina.

"Maybe," she said quietly, but still they heard her through the thick metal.

"Captain Michaels, we're here to rescue you. I need you to open this door."

"Captain?" Bryn said, confused.

"Yes," the voice responded.

"I'm not the captain." Bryn looked over at Amai.

"You are now." The man paused, and when he spoke again, he was unable to hide the irritation in his tone, "Listen, I need you to open this door. We can't override it."

"Right," Bryn said, but she didn't move. It would be simple to step forward and punch her code into the keypad. The doors would open and all of her precious air that she had worked so hard to save would rush out into the hallway, which would have depressurized hours ago at the rate of the leakage. She would collide with the figures in the hallway as all the tools she'd laid out on the floor rushed past them. And then they might pull a mask over her head and pump her full of pure oxygen as they crossed the bridge over to the Bernia. They'd get her clean clothes and she'd tell them about Tina. And of course, they would save her too—she'd be okay.

Or maybe when Bryn opened the door, and the disequilibrium forced her to crash into the bodies in the hallway, one of them would be holding a knife. Maybe they would slit her throat and clean up the remaining evidence that what happened to the Persika was anything but an accident. They'd take the disruptor from her body and when they found Tina, they'd kill her too.

Bryn fingered the disruptor she'd tucked away in her pocket and pulled it out. The blue light pulsed, as brilliant as the one she'd seen all those years ago in her parents' kitchen. It was always something that would have been beautiful if it didn't cause so much harm. Bryn closed her hands around the small ball and looked around her feet.

She was going to open the door. There were people outside of it that claimed they were there to help, and she had less than two hours of oxygen remaining. She had to take that chance. But she didn't have to have the disruptor with her when she pulled down her defenses. Bryn scanned the tools she laid out on the ground, looking for something to put it in. After trying to stuff it into freeze-dried food packages and under layers of cloth, Bryn emptied the emergency battery from a flashlight and stuck it inside. The light still pulsed through the thick plastic, but not enough to be seen once it was hidden amongst the wires under one of the floor panels, which she replaced hastily.

"Captain Michaels," the man in the hallway said. "Please just open the door. We're here to help."

Bryn wasn't sure if she imagined it, but the man's voice seemed to be growing softer—more friendly. Bryn allowed a small smile to spread across her lips. She zipped up her jumpsuit all the way to protect herself marginally against the bitter cold on the other side of the door, and then she stepped toward the doorway.

"Yes, I'm opening it now."

"Great," the voice replied, clearly relieved.

Bryn had already outstretched her arm toward the keypad when there was a soft beeping behind her.

Her limbs froze as her head turned around to glimpse the console. The soft beeping was unmistakable—it was the sound she'd been longing to hear for hours.

It was the sound of a message.

Bryn recoiled from the door and rushed to the console.

"Bryn!" the man yelled from the other side of the door, all his friendliness and understanding gone. "Open the goddamn door now!"

Bryn played the message so loudly that if Tina was awake, she would have been able to hear it all the way in the engine room. "This is Captain Nartu Umtuo of the Vernis responding to Bryn Michaels of the Persika. We have received your distress call and are en route to your location. We will arrive by 13:57, Earthtime. Hang in there, we're coming for you."

It was the message she'd been waiting for— the one she knew would come. She could have cried.

The message made her situation clear. The Persika was receiving just fine. The Bernia—or whatever ship it was hovering above her—wasn't trying to send any messages. The Bernia was trying to pretend like it wasn't even there.

Whoever was outside that door wasn't there to save her. They were there to kill her.

Bryn turned back around to face the door, but she stayed near the console. "Did you hear that? I don't need your help. You can leave!" Bryn said it cheerfully, almost offhandedly, as if their mere presence didn't terrify her to her core.

The voice on the other side of the door was grim, "You know we can't do that."

Bryn laughed. Why did she laugh?

"Why are you doing this?" Bryn finally asked when the laughter fell from her lips.

Once again there was a long silence on the other side of the door. The feet behind it began to shuffle through the bags of tools they'd brought with them. Bryn had no doubt that they were talking amongst themselves on a wavelength she couldn't hear.

Finally, he answered her, "We were ordered to."

"To kill me?" Bryn asked, her voice cracking.

"To tie up a loose end."

"I'm nothing," Bryn said, shaking her head. "*I'm nobody.* I don't understand. We didn't do anything wrong."

"I know," the voice said, "but you were caught in the crossfire." A small bit of sympathy had returned to his tone, but it was washed out by tools that clanged and sizzled against the metal of the door that Bryn refused to open.

In twenty-five minutes, the Vernis would be there to save her, but the man already on the ship would be through the door in less than ten. Bryn fidgeted with the knife in her pocket, but she continued to look around the cockpit for something more substantial. She opened cabinets hastily, wondering if she had missed a gun or a taser in her initial pass through. Unfortunately, she'd been thorough, and anything that might be of use was laid out on the floor in organized chaos.

Bryn picked up item after item, hoping she'd have a stroke of genius once it was in her hand, but food packets, batteries, and bandages were of little use in a combat situation, no matter how creative she tried to be. She realized that her best weapons would be her knife and her hands. There wasn't much she could do to improve the former, but when Bryn pulled out a syringe in the medical kit, she knew she could enhance the latter: there was a bottle of epinephrine.

Bryn stuck the needle into the syringe and drew the clear liquid out of the little bottle. She filled up the entire syringe, unsure if it was too much or too little, but she didn't have time to read the label. Sparks had begun to shoot from the frame of the door. They sizzled out before hitting the floor, but the tools were cutting through the metal, and Bryn sensed that they were almost through.

She held out her left arm and squeezed her hand into a fist, trying to get her veins to pop. She picked a thin blue line that ran through the underside of her elbow and pushed the tip of the needle under her skin.

There was the clang of metal on metal as they began to break down the door. It echoed throughout the cockpit so loudly that Bryn would have covered her ears if her hands weren't otherwise occupied.

She knew they were coming through, so she pushed the plunger down on the syringe and watched as the liquid disappeared into her arm. Bryn pulled the needle out of her skin and stood up. She staggered to the wall and wrapped her arms around a group of ropes tethered to the wall. Amai's sweet voice rang in her head, *"You should hold onto something."*

Bryn's heart started to race and her muscles twitched. A surge of energy welled within her body just as the door slid open, all of its intricate securities breached in less than eight minutes. The air was sucked from the cockpit as it mixed with the void outside of the door. All the loose items Bryn had pulled from the cockpit went with it, no doubt pelting the intruders who stood in the doorway. But Bryn stayed right where she was, holding onto the ropes.

The first figure through the door didn't stand a chance. He looked to his right, but Bryn was to his left. She brought her knife down on his neck and he was dead before he hit the floor. The second figure fared better, managing to pull the knife from Bryn's hand, but she threw enough hard punches that he fell to the ground, unmoving.

Pure energy flowed through Bryn's veins, and that was all she felt or thought. She didn't stop to consider her odds or try to reason with the figures that kept pouring through the door—she just kept fighting...at least until she ran out of air.

It didn't matter how much adrenaline was flowing through Bryn's veins. There wasn't enough oxygen in the air for her to fight. She gasped, trying to fill her lungs, but they remained empty. It felt like she was drowning.

Bryn fell to the floor, an involuntary hyperventilation causing her body to convulse. One figure stepped closer. His hand reached out to touch her cheek and the familiar voice said, "Where is it?"

She didn't answer. She couldn't even if she wanted to.

The voice grew harsher. Bryn looked up into his helmet, searching for his eyes, but all she saw was her own face reflected back at her. She looked tired and bloody—and scared. Bryn closed her eyes.

"Where's the disruptor?" he asked again, pulling her head up in his hands and shaking her, but Bryn hardly felt it at all.

Bryn smiled. There had been no way around it all along. She killed herself by trying to save herself. Amai was right again: they were already dead.

"Give her some oxygen," the voice hissed. One of the others brought over a canister with a mask attached to it. They hastily shoved it over Bryn's head and waited. They waited for her to breathe in. To fill anew with the hope of life. To tell them where she had hidden the evidence of their sins.

But Bryn didn't breathe in. She fought against every instinct in her body to keep herself from gasping for air. She laid perfectly still as her lungs screamed in agony and her eyes searched for any recognition of her former self in her reflection.

"Breathe, goddamnit!" the man yelled, shaking Bryn once again. He knew as well as Bryn that they didn't have enough time to search the entire cockpit before the Vernis arrived. They would leave empty handed if they couldn't pry it out of her.

Bryn could have breathed in. She wanted to breathe in...

But she was her father's daughter and she had promised herself she would go down fighting, so she didn't.

Made in the USA
Middletown, DE
15 February 2022